The Defender

by

Herman L. Jimerson

PublishAmerica
Baltimore

© 2009 by Herman L. Jimerson.
All rights reserved. No part of this book may be reproduced, stored in a retrieval system or transmitted in any form or by any means without the prior written permission of the publishers, except by a reviewer who may quote brief passages in a review to be printed in a newspaper, magazine or journal.

First printing

All characters in this book are fictitious, and any resemblance to real persons, living or dead, is coincidental.

PublishAmerica has allowed this work to remain exactly as the author intended, verbatim, without editorial input.

ISBN: 1-60813-428-8
PUBLISHED BY PUBLISHAMERICA, LLLP
www.publishamerica.com
Baltimore

Printed in the United States of America

Dedication

This book is dedicated to all of the people who have contributed to my life, well-being, and happiness; to those who have helped me in pursuit of the cause; and to all attorneys who have devoted themselves for the purpose of upholding the Constitution, and not allowing themselves to be corrupted by money and power. This book is especially dedicated to my wife Laura, my mother, and my dear grandmother for their life-long support. I would also like to thank my son Lee for his encouragement and support.

Preface

The Defender is a book devoted to exposing the true fight for the common good in a legal world that is often legally blind and indifferent. In the midst of darkness and depravity, there are still those attorneys who value all life and try to make a difference however and wherever they can. This book is far from the realms of silk purse, money-driven attorneys and dives deep into the heart where law really counts: helping the underprivileged and revealing the corruption in very high places built into a system that most people trust.

It is hoped that readers will be enlightened and inspired as attorney Drew Jones leads them on a compelling path encountering love, hate, good, evil, darkness, depravity, racism, and romance. *The Defender* is a beacon of light that shatters the traditions of the way things are always done. Drew Jones is a one-of-a-kind black attorney who is about to leave the white strong hold establishment spinning on its heels. *The Defender* is based on the true story of the life of Attorney Herman Jimerson.

Acknowledgement

Thanks to Linda Leon and Karen Peralta for helping me to birth this dream.

Chapter 1

Drew Jones pushed himself away from the table. He leaned back in the worn leather chair taking a reprieve from the books that had become his obsession. They were two huge books, reminding him of the tablets of stone Moses brought down from the mountain after his encounter with God—and they were that serious. These days, the table, the books, and the chair were taking all of his time. They had spent many intense nights together, almost like lovers. They demanded all of him. Although he would have gladly traded them in for a woman's touch, a promise that he made to his family kept him tied to the chair, and his own pleasures would have to wait.

In a fleeting thought, he recalled his father's strong hands, blistered from pounding railroad spikes onto the ties. In his small backwards town that is all you could do: pound nails or pick cotton in the hellish Missouri sun. Perhaps it was the pounding of the rain against his window that took him back to his father. "Drew, take this water to your father," his mind reflected as his mother handed him a jug. Once again he was in the small town of Sikeston, Missouri. He saw himself riding his bike with a partially frozen gallon of water in the aluminum basket that was mounted to the handle bars of his bike. That was one of his jobs every summer, to take his father water. He recalled the smell of sweat and sound of labor. It was about seventy men. All singing the same tune, pounding spikes in rhythm. He knew his own hands would never see that kind of toil. As a child he had already rejected the thought of it.

His father smiled as he saw him approaching. The bike slowed down as the tires rolled off the asphalt trail to gravel. The wheels spun dust and tiny rocks as he pumped hard to reach his destination. The tracks were quite depressing to Drew. The men always looked so worn and tired. The area was dusty; hot iron tracks were piled up for what seemed like miles to be repaired, and the smell of laboring men was awful.

Upon reaching his father, Drew dismounted the bike and brought the jug over. His father did the same thing every time. He greeted him kindly, then pulled off his cap and poured the water over his head before taking a chug.

One thing that always stood out to Drew was how content his father seemed. Whenever he visited the tracks he could always hear people complaining. They would talk about it being too hot, or curse the fact that they had to work at such a dismal place. He never heard his father complain at work or at home. He was grateful to have a job.

His father's life was propelled by labor. In his generation, a tool in your hand was the only way to survive. Success was merely the possession of a job. Drew determined that his hands would never touch a tool. They would touch books, taking him places far beyond his father's world and leading him to where success comes through bringing dreams to life.

This was quite an odd yet revolutionary thought to some in his family. Didn't he understand that this was a white man's world? But he would always silence those voices with his grandmothers' words: "Your life is meant to be something, Drew." The rain continued to lull Drew into memories of his childhood. The smell of his grandmother's hot buttered rolls and southern cooking and her gentle voice were all etched in his memory.

For just a few moments he saw his grandmother again. She was short and a little stocky. Her skin was dark, and her hair was long and silver. A long cotton dress was covered by the white apron she always wore in the kitchen. As much as she cooked you would have thought that apron would be covered with splatters. But it was not. She was a neat cook. She always put things away quickly after she used them and always had a wet rag on hand to wipe away anything that did splatter. Grandma was proud of her cooking and did a superb job at it. He had gained so many life lessons from her just sitting around the table as she cooked.

"Drew," she would say, "unless you have given everything that you've got, you haven't done anything. Anybody can do just enough, but people that do all that they can, succeed and benefit others."

At that moment a flash of lightning and roar of thunder filled the room. His mind shifted again. This time he was standing in the rain watching his grandmother's coffin being lowered into the ground. With that, part of his life was being buried too. His heart ached. He vowed never to forget the wisdom that she had imparted to him. He would live by Grandma's creed—hard work, dedication, and the pursuit of doing what is right. As his mind scanned his past, he recalled the empty feeling of not having his mother at the funeral, because she had preceded his grandmother in death. She had died of lung cancer a few years before.

From an early age, Drew learned never to give up. He came from the womb trying to survive as severe asthma almost ended his life. He was the sixth child born of his mother. Three of his siblings were stillborn. His family knew that it was not a twist of fate that he was one of the survivors. His grandma used to say, the fact he survived and all his talk about wanting to go to school and not work on the tracks or the cotton field were somehow mixed into a divine mission from God. Somehow, his family came to accept that trading a tool for a book was expected of him. Drew indeed would break the traditions of his forefathers.

Slowly, he pulled his mind away from his memories. Now the rain sounded more like the beating of a kettle drum, pounding even harder and rhythmically reminding him: get back to work, get back to work. His hand reached for the books, and his mind resumed studying for the bar. Nothing in life was more serious than this.

Law school had been tough. But Drew's desire to become a lawyer was stronger than death. It had to be. Dreams often died in his world. Being an African American in a small racist town where the railroad tracks literally split the white and black sections of town in two was a reality he refused to conform to.

Drew's mother moved from Sikeston to St. Louis before he reached his teens. He always hated that his parent's marriage failed. Living in the inner city was a rude awakening for him. Not only did he have to fight to preserve his dream. He had to fight to stay alive. Too many young black males had fallen prey to drugs and alcohol while living in the projects. He attributed his survival to his mother's strong faith in God and her tough disposition. She did not let her kids get away with anything. They were held accountable, and she pushed them to do well.

Freedom that lay just beyond the bar exam was well in sight for Drew. Even though Grandma and Mother would never see it, his promise to become a lawyer would be fulfilled. In his heart, somewhere in eternity he knew they would know about it and rejoice with him. The closer he came to the exam, he could feel success. It was imminent. Law was freedom to Drew. It was his destiny, and nothing could stop him.

Chapter 2

Drew opened his refrigerator, only to be greeted by a few cans of beer and some left-over pizza. That would just have to do for breakfast. It would be so good to have a pay check right about now. Days like this reminded him of the sacrifices he made to become a lawyer. He clearly understood the power of choice recalling prior to his law school days working twelve to fifteen hours daily dealing with people at the local halfway house. These people had made very poor choices. A halfway house is really a nice name for a federal inmate holding pen for criminals before they are released back into society, often unreformed, leaving them wide open to make even more wrong choices.

Really, it should be called the revolving door because the state doesn't care: inmate in, inmate out, inmate back in—just more money for the system. But, for some strong reason, Drew felt very connected to the people, and he worked very hard to help anybody that he could. Bad choices made Drew think about his brother…

"DeMarcus! Don't do it, DeMarcus!"

"Shut up, Drew. I'm not going to let some punk beat up on me. See this, Drew, see this tooth! We don't have money to go to no dentist." For DeMarcus a missing tooth was disastrous. He had prided himself on his good looks. He needed all of his teeth. That dazzling smile was part of his prowess.

Drew's mind drifted back to the strong reason that propelled his destiny. His brother was the primary inspiration for this strong reason. DeMarcus was Drew's older brother, the fireball of the family, always getting into something. This day it was over Rita, a teenage boy's fantasy but supposedly off limits to him. DeMarcus was not going to let any body tell him whom he could or could not have.

"Put the gun back! Put it back!"

DeMarcus pushed Drew onto his mother's bed, cocked the .22 caliber pistol, and went to make his hell-raising statement at school. Thank God somebody spotted the pistol and reported it, thus avoiding a blood bath.

This choice was the beginning of DeMarcus troubled life and Drew's legal career. DeMarcus was arrested and sent to juvenile detention to await trial for possession of a gun. Just as the tracks in the town separated whites from blacks, they also mentally separated those that would succeed in life and those that would fail. At that point, Drew and his brother determined which side of the track would dominate their lives. It was clear from DeMarcus's lack of remorse that his life would be spent on the failure side. Drew's mother was devastated and spent all she had getting her son out of harm's way. She spent her last dime hiring James Arrington, an aged and highly professional black lawyer.

Drew watched as his mother cried telling Arrington the story. He noticed the lawyer responding in such a calm and compassionate manner. It was profoundly moving for Drew, almost mesmerizing. He had never seen a lawyer of any kind. But surely all lawyers were white. Surely there was not a black attorney doing business in the Boot Heels of Missouri. Was this some dream? It wasn't.

Drew later learned that Arrington was a very affluent lawyer, highly successful in civil rights litigation in St. Louis, and nationally known. In trial, he was a genius. He practiced family law and made himself available for this case. Drew watched as he powerfully presented his case. His brilliant oratory could only leave one option for the judge—dismissal. *I'm going to be a lawyer*, Drew thought to himself. This encounter had forever changed his life. It was the seed that took him to the other side of the tracks.

It wasn't long before DeMarcus made a return trip to the court house. He had not learned a thing. He was arrested again for a fight over the same girl, Rita. She must have been his first because he was fighting over her like a ram bucking for mating rights. This was insane.

"What the hell are you doing, DeMarcus?" his mother screamed, "Fighting over some damn girl again. Have you lost your mind? Look, I don't have no money this time. You know how hard it was for me to get that lawyer? I'm still paying him, and now this! I can't help you! I just can't help you!"

Drew could see the agony in his mother's face. A part of her wanted to administer tough love and yet a part of her was dying on the inside because she wished she had the money to help her baby. She did not want to see her baby go to jail. She did not want to see her baby become another statistic in the projects. But this was inner city life, and not many mothers were spared this chapter. Some mothers had even buried their babies. In tears she said, "Drew, I can't go to court. I can't watch. Go with your brother when he has to go to court." He was hurting so badly for his mother and felt like knocking some sense into DeMarcus for being such a dumb ass.

This turned out to be another fateful choice. Drew's court appearance with DeMarcus would forever seal his destiny and validate for life his divine mission. It was a crowded courtroom, Division 26, the initial door for every state offender living in St. Louis. It was hot and stuffy. Hard wooden benches were the home for everyone for the next few hours who had in one way or another offended the state of Missouri. The clerks were busy sorting dockets.

The clerk called the trial docket: "State vs. DeMarcus Jones." This was the first time DeMarcus had ever shown any emotion. He was actually afraid. Drew jumped up beside him as they walked to the bench.

Before anybody could say anything, Drew blurted out, "We move for the dismissal of this case."

The judge, hearing a voice but seeing no one, leaned over the bench and smiled. "Who are you?"

"Drew Jones."

"Are you an attorney?"

"No, Judge, but I'm going to be."

The judge was pleasantly and surprisingly moved. This was the first time Drew had announced to the world with such clarity that he wanted to be something. He was twelve years old at the time.

"Well, Mr. DeMarcus Jones, you have an outstanding attorney; please help him in becoming one. I feel he would make a great attorney. Case dismissed." Everyone in the courtroom got a chuckle out of this, including the prosecutor who would not dare steal this show.

Drew had won his first case without even going to law school. He could have died and gone to heaven. He had spoken up for someone who was in no position to speak for himself. This would be his trademark in the legal world. And, as far as Drew was concerned, the judge was an angel of justice. He would never know his name, but would never forget him.

THE DEFENDER

Drew became a neighborhood hero, and from that time on, he was destined to help many people. Some of the very same people who applauded him as a child would end up at the halfway house. Amidst the people murdering, beatings, rape, and people incarcerated for the most trivial incidents were those who remembered Drew's choice and encouraged him to pursue law school. They encouraged him to do some good in his life and not to make the same terrible choices that they had that led them into a life of chaos.

Chapter 3

Drew had stepped over the tracks by taking the bar exam. He knew that in order to stay there he had to find a job. Most people would have waited for the results first, but not Drew. He knew he had passed, so he went out looking for work. He was even cocky enough to demand a $48,000-a-year salary. Of course, that was met by much ridicule from those who waited for their results.

A head lawyer from a small black legal firm just scoffed at him for exuding such confidence. Drew just moved on from that place. The "good ole boys club" at the St. Louis Prosecutor's Office had already put the discretionary word out that unless you had blue-blooded connections, which was the code for anything non-white, don't even bother applying. He applied anyway. *Drew vividly remembered the day District Attorney Payton Hill turned him down for the job. "Mr. Jones, we appreciate you taking the time to apply to the prosecutor's office, but we don't have any positions open at the time. However, we will keep your résumé on file and if anything comes available we will notify you,"* Drew nodded and then got up to leave. *Something on the inside told him don't say anything. You knew this was going to happen anyway. But Drew could not resist the other side saying show him the paper. "Can I help you with something else, Mr. Jones?" "I was just curious as to why this ad is running in yesterday's* Legal Advocate *newspaper that the district attorney's office was hiring?" "Let me see that, Mr. Jones."*

Drew passed him the paper. "You know what, I'm sure we cancelled that ad but sometimes it takes about a week to get it pulled from the paper."

"I understand," Drew said. The reason Drew's memory was so vivid is that he always read the *Legal Advocate* and the ad ran for at least two months after his interview with Payton Hill.

Then he applied at the Public Defender's Office, charged with handling all cases where the defendant could not afford a lawyer. Blake Adams, a brilliant chief defense attorney, scheduled an interview with Drew.

Drew walked into the large room and sat down at the spacious oval table. This was going to be a six-panel interview, something that he had not anticipated. Nobody feels comfortable with six people firing out all kinds of questions, but, with each round of successful answers, Drew grew more confident. He was honored to be in the room with people that had reputations of power.

Blake Adams was a figure larger than life. He was known for being fair, a legal mastermind, and an avid newspaper reader, which made him quite the talk of the office. It was a legend that he read every newspaper in the country. The fact was he was a very avid reader and at least ten newspapers from all parts of the country crossed his desk every day. He was well loved and respected because he cared for his office, the attorneys and, most important, the clients. In this very racist town, Blake was a white diamond. His assistant Calvin Row was a perfect complement. He had a mind for detail and was considered one of the best lawyers in St. Louis. If you ever needed a judge or a jury to do "the right thing," he was the man to do the persuading.

The other panel members were Ashley Hill, Katherine Miles, and Jeffrey Ellis. These people would be the foundation of Drew's career as a defender. Jeffrey Ellis was later to be Drew's team leader. He would eventually be promoted to the first African American Chief Justice of the Missouri Supreme Court.

As the attorneys continued firing questions, Ashley Hill asked one that Drew knew could either make or break his desired career as a defender. "Drew, what would cause you to leave the Public Defenders?" Drew thought for a quick minute, and, just as abruptly as the little boy who stood before the judge, blurted, "I would leave if someone came in and shot the place up with a machine gun, but they would have to do it twice." This was a career-making answer; the room exploded with laughter—he was in.

Unexpected late night calls have very few purposes. In Drew's mind, they were either to announce death or some other tragic event. He rolled out of bed, dragged himself to the kitchen telephone, and braced himself for the unpleasant news. Glancing at the clock on the wall, he noticed that it was after midnight on October 1.

"May I speak to Drew?"

He almost felt like lying and saying he wasn't at home to avoid the unwanted news. "This is Drew," he said.

"Drew, this is Blake Adams. First, I want to congratulate you on passing the bar, and, second, I want to offer you a job at the Public Defender's Office."

Drew was speechless and asked Blake to repeat it. The late hour caused him to doubt his own ears. Before Blake could finish saying it, though, Drew said a resounding yes.

"Fine, come in Monday morning, and we will get you going."

This was overwhelming. He had passed the bar exam and secured his position beyond the tracks all in one night. Drew wept. This was the happiest day of his life and the saddest, because those he had made the promise to were no longer there. Death had separated them. He would have given anything to see their eyes and experience their joy. But, in a surreal moment, he could almost see them and certainly he could hear them saying,

THE DEFENDER

"I knew you would make it. We told you that you were special."

He never expected it to be like this. This announcement should be accompanied by at least a dinner celebration. But he was standing in his underwear at his window looking with great joy and great apprehension into tomorrow. He did not even have anyone special in his life that he could call. So it was just him, his tears, and his memories. And, of course, there was the always near-empty refrigerator. He reached in, grabbed a beer, and toasted himself to the future and all that would come.

Chapter 4

Drew was out of bed the next morning before the sun rose. He thought he would need a wake-up call from his nieces, Stephanie and Shauna, but the adrenaline of that life-changing moment was so high that he barely slept. He kept staring at the "twin commandments"—those huge law books that he had so diligently applied himself to. Today, knowledge and application would merge. He felt like he was coming off the mountain to serve the people just like Moses. The two stone tablets of the Ten Commandments contained all the law the people needed; he knew those books had all the laws the people of the state of Missouri needed. Today was his day to begin putting the laws into practice.

He thought about what grandma would say if she could see him, and, as he lifted the leather briefcase that his mother had given him years before her death, he felt tears welling in his eyes. "Baby, now, when you have your first case, be sure to take this with you," he could hear his mother say. It was one of the most expensive things that she had ever bought. She had invested in his future because she knew he was going to make it.

Drew knew that it did not take much to make him feel important because he had so little. Today, it only took the black Sunday suit that his grandmother had given him and his mother's briefcase. Nobody would ever know he didn't have two nickels in his pocket and that the briefcase only contained a sack lunch of a bologna sandwich and some Cheese Nips. When he left for the bus that morning, he was on top of the world. Within a week, he found himself quite a part of the St. Louis bus culture and was getting the reputation of a crowd-warmer.

As the bus rocked and rolled over the tracks, Drew said to himself, "I have finally made it to the Promised Land." He could see old dilapidated buildings, the homeless awakening from their night under the bridge, and the housing projects that had long been un-kept. Slowly those images faded into his Promised Land of huge sky-scraping glass buildings, large department stores, and corner restaurants. Everything seemed brighter and better. Even the trash on the street looked better than where he was from. He felt like the ugly little worm that, in just a moment, had a metamorphosis into an elaborate, complex butterfly.

He rang for his stop and with great confidence walked across the street into the large tan marble building that housed the Public Defender's system. He would quickly learn that it was a very efficient place that wasted nothing, especially manpower and time. It took just one day for Drew to be assigned his first case by Blake Adams. Now he really had something to put in that brief case: the story of a man who had been sitting in jail for six months and for something that you would not believe. Somehow, it did not surprise Drew that that man who had been in jail for six months and had never even been given his rights was black.

As he walked through the halls of the county jail, he saw that it was all disproportionately black. It wasn't long before he evidenced that blacks and poor people always got the most severe punishment for crimes and ambition. He could not help notice how some whites would come in with a DWI charge and be released on probation, while blacks facing the same charge had to spend time in county jail. Or how certain white professionals would face drug charges such as possession of cocaine and get a far lighter sentence than blacks using crack that is made from the same substance. But the cases that always disheartened Drew were black professionals who had made some infraction against the law and were charged with the full measure of the law despite their otherwise outstanding reputations when the range of punishment allowed for leniency. He had watched many blacks damage their careers over felony charges that could have been reduced to misdemeanors or dropped. His client was just one of many. He was apprehended for what white people would never have faced court over.

"Good morning, Mr. Bostick," said Drew. "Sorry that you've been here quite a while with no representation."

Gino Bostick was a dark-skinned, kind of disheveled-looking man. His speech was poor, but his emotions could be clearly read.

"I didn't know what to do, sir; I just needed some gas."

"So you passed off the two dollar bill for a twenty." Gino didn't respond.

"I am going to take your case, Gino; I just need to know what happened."

"You don't know nothing about being broke, so you probably won't understand." Drew wanted to tell him so much but that was not what he was there to do. It's amazing how a black suit can cause a person to assume so much. He just listened.

"I lost my job, and I don't have no money. I knew I couldn't really look for a job if I didn't have gas, and the bus doesn't run everywhere. I begged the guy for just a tank of gas and promised to give him the money back. But he wouldn't do it…"

"So you passed off the two dollar bill."

"I was desperate, man. Are you going to help me?"

"You have a right to a fair trial. I will be there for you." This made Drew an instant hit with Gino.

Gino had performed an old con artist, but people will do anything when they are desperate enough. In that case, the legal system is blind, rarely considering the cause and effect of a situation. It is almost as if the slightest offense deserves the full measure of the law. In Gino's case, a slighted law caused the St. Louis police department to beat a confession out him. Drew was determined to fight this case to the extreme; no one should have to rot in jail over a two dollar bill scam.

The trial was scheduled within a week in front of Judge Gavin Bishop. He was a brilliant jurist, known to be fair and decent. The office had a policy that the first two jury trials had to be second seated by a senior attorney. Calvin Row chose to second seat Drew's trials. This was an excellent set up for Drew—a fair judge and a senior attorney who knew how to get people to do the right thing.

"The attorney that you will be going up against in this case is Anthony Hollis. He is a pretty cold character," Calvin said.

"Why do you say that?"

"Let me just be honest about my observations, and you can take it for what it's worth. He has a way of insulting your intelligence and he's been known to bribe police officers. That's not good. I don't know what it is about the prosecutor's office, but the more of an ass you are, the faster you get promoted. He's pretty high up on the chain. All I can conclude is that he acts that way because he knows how their system of promotion works. I'm just giving you this information because the first time he said something derogatory towards me it was in the middle of a trial, and it threw my game off. What made me even angrier is that the judge didn't say anything about his behavior."

"This is such a simple case, so he probably won't have that opportunity on this one, but it is good to be informed."

"You're right. Just go in there and do a good job. If he says anything you will be one step ahead of him. Another thing that has helped me tremendously along the way is to sit in on trials and just watch how attorneys operate. It will help you to be prepared. In this job you have to have the knowledge, but you also have to be part drama. Anthony Hollis is good at drama."

The jury was selected. This is always difficult because the average citizen always seems to believe the worst about the defendant. One juror said, "He got locked up, so he must already be guilty." The good old faith-building adage, in the court of law you are innocent until proven guilty, is a joke. But it is good propaganda which allows "the system" to do business as usual with all the corruption that John Q. Public never would even perceive. The prevailing attitude among non-lawyers, especially white ones, is that the police can do no wrong, and their testimony is always as pure as the Pope's.

The attorney's began their opening statements. The prosecutor called Albert Martinez, the cashier that was on duty that day.

"Mr. Martinez, where were you located inside the store when you observed the defendant?"

"I was standing behind the counter near the cash register."

"What did you observe outside the store?"

"People were filling up their cars. Then I saw a very dark black person."

"Is the person that you saw in the courtroom today?"

"Yeah, the black guy sitting at the table, next to that white guy."

"What did he do?"

"He put twenty dollars of gas in the car and tried to pass off a two-dollar bill for a twenty-dollar. I said this ain't no twenty."

"What happened next?"

"He just left."

"No further questions."

Drew began his cross-examination of the witness.

"Mr. Martinez, do you always make it a habit to only identify black customers as they come into the establishment."

"No sir."

"You told the prosecutor that there were other person's filling up their cars, but you noticed the black man."

"Well, um...I did not mean it like that."

"What other nationalities did you see that day?"

"I wasn't paying any particular attention..."

"But you noticed the black man?"

He was silent for a moment. "Please answer the question yes or no."

"Yes."

"You stated that the defendant passed off a two-dollar bill instead of a twenty-dollar."

"Yes."

"Was he the only person in line that day?"

"I don't remember."

"So there is a possibility that someone else in line could have given you the two-dollar bill."

"No I spoke to him."

"But you said he just left, maybe he did not know you were talking to him since he did not respond."

"But..."

"Mr. Martinez, you stated that the defendant was very dark. I do not think that most people would consider that person very dark."

"Objection."

"Sustained, Mr. Jones please keep comments relevant."
"No further questions."
The D.A. called his next witness, Officer Dangerfield.
"Officer Dangerfield, how long have you been on the force?"
"Ten years."
"Have you made many arrests?"
"Probably hundreds."
"Are you trained to identify suspects?"
"Yes."
"Tell us, Officer Dangerfield, what you did."
"I received a radio dispatch for a theft at Exxon Gas Station and responded. I interviewed Mr. Martinez, and he told me that a black male, six feet tall weighing about one hundred forty-five pounds stole gas and attempted to pass a two-dollar bill for a twenty-dollar."
"Did the cashier give you a physical description of the car?"
"Yes, he didn't get the license plates, but said it was a light blue Chevy Nova."
"What did you do next?"
"I drove around and observed the neighborhood for cars fitting that description being drove by a black male."
"What happened next?"
"I spotted a car fitting the description on 14th Street driving at a high rate of speed with a missing tail light. I turned on my emergency lights and pursued. The vehicle stopped. It looked like the description of the male so I took him back to the store for identification."
"Where did you have him identified?"
"It was in the backseat of my patrol car in handcuffs. The cashier said that was him."
"No further questions."
Drew began to cross-examine Officer Dangerfield.

"Was the only place available to identify the defendant the back seat of the police car?"

"No."

"Could you have asked the defendant to step outside of the car in order to get a more accurate identification?"

"Yes."

"Were you one of the officers that booked and interviewed Mr. Bostick in the county jail?"

"Did Mr. Bostick confess to passing the two-dollar bill?"

"Yes."

"Was Mr. Bostick under any duress when he made his confession?"

"I don't know how he was emotionally at the time."

"Let me rephrase the question. Do you recognize the man in this picture?"

"Yes."

"Is it the defendant?"

"Yes."

"Do you notice that the man in this picture has been severely beaten and that these pictures were taken directly after his interrogation?"

"Yes."

"Now, do you think Mr. Bostick could have been under duress when he made his confession?"

"I assume that is possible."

"Prior to the beating, according to Mr. Martinez's report, the defendant did not respond to the accusation against him and that is what you wrote in your police report, correct?

"Yes."

"No further questions."

Knowing that the art of defense is part drama in his closing argument, he called the police officer a liar and a bully. Could any police force be trusted for beating a confession out of a man? Was the man telling the truth, or was he just agreeing to stop them from beating the shit out of him? With all the money that convenience stores collect by the hour, who could really identify that it was Gino who passed off the two dollar bill anyway? Was it simply just another, "the black man did it" thing? The only description of the perpetrator was that he was a very dark, tall black man. Drew pointed out that Gino was not as dark as the clerk had told the police and suggested that the prosecutor really did not care because all they wanted was to put another man in jail. Drew fought hard in this trial and made passionate arguments for Gino. He had punched holes into the prosecutor's game, but was it enough?

The jury deliberated for six hours. Drew knew he had punched some pretty good holes, but it was not enough. It was a bittersweet moment for Drew. He wanted an acquittal. But he got the next best thing: a defender's victory. This is when the defendant is not acquitted, but, at the same time, he does not get the full measure of the law. The jury recommended that Gino only spend two days in county jail. Though Drew was devastated when he heard the verdict, Gino was smiling and said the sweetest words any defense attorney wants to hear: "Thanks for fighting for me." For Drew this was still as precious as gold because a desperate man would not have his life crushed by the full force of law.

Everyone in the courthouse knew a defender's victory was still a significant victory, though less than an acquittal. Besides, Gino was going home because he had already spent six months behind bars. Calvin, the senior attorney, tried to lighten Drew's mood. "You know, Gino was kind of dark." The two attorneys laughed. Gino and Drew became friends, and soon he was one of the most-requested attorneys. Word gets around quickly when people know you care.

Chapter 5

It's amazing how angels work. They are as busy as lawyers. DeMarcus' angel was a judge sitting on a bench. Maurita Middleton's angel was a fiery church lady named Sister Elena. Blake Adams had assigned Drew the Middleton case after a call from Sister Elena requesting him as the defense attorney. This streetwise Pentecostal preacher was always about intervention. Sister Elena had a heart for prostitutes. She knew Middleton was a woman of the night and had always tried to redirect her misguided life.

Drew met Middleton in his office. He looked at this frail woman who had the apparent markings of one familiar with drugs. She had the trapping of a street woman on—dress high, tight, and revealing. Her hair was dark, short, and perfectly complementing her milk chocolate weathered skin. Drew could see something trapped under all the layers of makeup. It came out through her bewildered yet pleading eyes. What was this woman's story? He did not believe it was going to be the typical prostitution case—the kind where you ask the judge for leniency and keep the prostitute out of jail.

"I never wanted to be here," Middleton said.

"You mean arrested."

"No, I mean in this life."

Drew knew it was his business to get to the point, but somehow he felt drawn to hear this woman out. Not many prostitutes would talk about anything for fear of their pimp. So Middleton was either crazy or wanted to get out.

"You know why I hate the color pink?" At this point Drew did not know if the drugs were talking or was it Middleton. "I hate pink. 'Cause my mama made me wear it every time she ran out of money for drugs. 'Little girls look pretty in pink,' she would say. I want you to look pretty for John."

Drew began to cringe. "Miss Middleton, maybe we should get to the issues at hand."

"This is the issue, Mr. Jones. John raped me when I was seven years old. He was my mother's boyfriend, and every time I had to wear the pink gown. That's how she paid for her fix. She would sit outside the door hearing me scream."

Drew could see that Middleton was reliving incidents in her mind. He could see it in her face on every pause of conversation. "How long did this go on, Miss Middleton?"

"It has not stopped yet, Mr. Jones. It has never ended. I just went from my mother's bedroom to the street. I tried to get help...I tried to tell my school counselor something. But when my mother found out about it, she pulled me out of school and told them she was home schooling me. Nobody ever tried to find out anything more about the little girl who always cried at school. The worse my mother's habit got, the more I was screwed, but this time by lots of different men. It's a sick world, Mr. Jones."

Drew stared into her grimacing face. He knew there was very little he could do but listen. "Did you ever try to escape?

"And go where? It's only one time that I thought I was about to get out of this life."

"When was that?"

"That's when the cops did a drug bust in my mother's apartment. They busted in and arrested my mother. I remember them yelling and screaming, then they kicked in the door where I was. It didn't take them very long to figure out what I was used for. The man I was with jumped out the window. I just balled up in the sheets on the bed. I thought they were going to arrest me too, but they didn't. Sometimes I wished to God that they would have."

"What happened?"

"One of the officers that made the raid got a good look at me. He went away with the other officers, but, a few days later, he came back knowing that I was alone and raped me."

Drew was sick with disgust.

"He made me do unspeakable things, Mr. Jones, and since there were no records on me because of "home schooling," he turned me out on the streets with a pimp that he was connected with. I am a sex slave, Mr. Jones, and I'd rather be dead. Lee Vincent is a bastard…"

Drew was shocked. "Did you say Officer Lee Vincent?"

"He's not an officer, Mr. Jones; he's a bastard."

Drew was new to this but never would have imagined anything so corrupt. He thought this mess only happened in movies. He was right in the middle of a St. Louis scandal. By exposing the police department he would be cutting off his own head. He sat there just trying to take this all in.

Filing a formal complaint to Internal Affairs on behalf of Middleton was the match that would ignite the inferno Drew knew he was walking into. Nobody crossed the St. Louis police—they were as deadly as the mafia except with a smile. The general public was duped into believing that they were its finest citizens. But those who had encountered the men in blue knew better. It wouldn't take long for word to spread throughout the court that Drew had every intention of entering Dante's gates of hell.

Just as Drew expected, Internal Affairs did nothing with the complaint other than to acknowledge it. He moved on to the chief prosecutor Payton Hill. Drew entered his lush office. You would have thought you had entered the halls of royalty. Everything was perfectly decorated—mahogany furniture, red carpet, and crystal and silver awards on the desk; the walls were studded with accolades.

"Drew, do you really think Middleton is giving you the facts here or this bull shit because she got arrested?" Hill asked.

"You think that she would risk her life telling me this?"

"Listen, Vincent is one of the most respected officers on the force; all this is going to do is stir up a bunch of mess. You better have something more substantial than what you're telling me if you think I'm going to put my name on it. You're new here, and one thing you are going to have to learn is that we don't prosecute everything."

Drew leaned over Hill's desk and glared at him, "Are you telling me that you've already made your decision, without looking over the information? My client has filed an assault, rape and human trafficking complaint, sir."

Hill slowly tipped himself back in his chair. "Well, it looks like I will just have to become more informed over this matter." He reached over and pulled the report from Drew's hand. Drew knew Hill had something to hide. He was more than likely even one of the clients.

As Drew was leaving Hill's office, Hill called out, "Hey fellow, just one piece of advice: not everything about St. Louis law is written in the books. *Sometimes the things we pursue only come to a dead end.*"

Drew didn't bother to respond. It was already an established fact that the court and police systems were like magicians: they could make all kinds of things disappear. Drew was determined not to walk in fear. He proceeded to build his case, pulling over five years of prostitution arrest records on Vincent and filed motion after motion citing constitutional violation including criminal extortion and white slavery. They had violated her right to an attorney and rights against cruel and unusual punishment. Finally Judge Eric Saxon was assigned the case. The Middleton case was set for immediate trial on Monday morning. This was a good way for Drew to end the week; finally something was done.

Drew stopped by to visit Middleton before he left the office. Even the county jail was buzzing about a prostitute getting the opportunity to go to trial and actually be properly defended.

"We might not get a snowball's chance in hell," Middleton said, "But I sure thank you for helping me, even if I don't get a chance to see it."

Drew looked at Middleton, puzzled. "What do you mean?"

"This is street life, Mr. Jones. People die and are never heard of again. It's just the way things are."

"Are you afraid to die? I'm not."

"I used to be, but Sister Elena said that God was only a prayer away and that he will listen to us even beyond our last breath. She said after you take your last breath down here, that is when you take your first breath in heaven and you will be with him forever."

Drew envisioned his grandmother telling him about Jesus when he was a little boy for just a moment. She had painted a picture of heaven too, but not as simple and beautiful as this one. Her picture was of the joy of pearly gates and golden streets, not death that leads you into eternity.

"How long have you known the Lord?"

"Since Sister Elena taught me about him a long time ago. All I said was Jesus come into my heart. I remember her jumping up and down saying, 'You got it! You got it!' She was one of the first persons that I met when Vincent put me out on the streets. She's always been there for me. That's my angel."

Drew left the county jail that day overwhelmed and amazed at the precious treasure found in things life considers trash.

The Jury Room was the local haunt of lawyers. It was the place where nobodies became somebodies, and the somebodies moved up the professional chain just a little higher. Careers began and ended here.

Tonight was Drew's night. Many people shook his hand and wished him good luck. He knew what was about to happen was a big deal, but, by the response of the crowd, he knew he had underestimated how big the deal was. He could sense that many well wishers had an ulterior motive; they had bet money, because many of these same friendly faces had never even once acknowledged him in the halls of the court house. He wondered what the bet was. Would he lose? Would he win? Or would he be killed?

"The drinks are on us, Drew," the bartender said, handing him a beer. Drew looked around the room. *This is really something*, he thought to himself. In the corner, he could see a few detectives glancing over at him in disdain. *To hell with them*, he thought, *they've got it coming*.

Drew sat for a while watching a few couples whiz about on the dance floor. He kept himself entertained by all of the random chatter with some colleagues and even enjoyed watching some of the tight shirt judges come out of their boxes. To Drew, the Jury Room was a place he had to frequently check in to stay "in." He had learned that much of the game. Social climbing meant checking in at least enough for the bartender to know you personally and the regulars to consider you a regular. For Drew this was a few times a month. Other than that, it was a place quite filled with people who often put on a show for public justice, but abused their positions of power. The Middleton case had already exposed more than what he wished to know about. Drew had a name for those type people: jackasses. After downing a few more complimentary beers, Drew decided to check out.

The freezing St. Louis air brought any sobering necessary to Drew. As he walked to his car that was parked two blocks away, he recalled the events of the day and especially his conversation with Middleton. This was all so worth it. A homeless person saw him passing and called out, "Got any spare change?" This night Drew was in a very benevolent mood, grateful for the opportunity to help one more person. He checked his pocket and handed the man a five dollar bill. The man nodded his thanks.

For some reason, Drew noticed more homeless than usual. Perhaps it was the chilling weather that made him notice how so many of them were huddled under flimsy cardboard boxes wearing only the thinnest of apparel. As he approached his car, he saw two men standing near his trunk arguing. *This is a bad night for these homeless people. I wish I could do something,* he thought.

One was a tall, thin white guy with a red bandanna wrapped around his head. The other was a medium-built black guy whom apparently no one had informed that it was freezing outside. He just stood there swearing in his jeans and white T-shirt. The white guy lifted up a brown paper bag as if to take a swig of something.

"Excuse me, man; do you have a light?" the white guy said.

"Sure man." Drew reached in his pocket to pull the lighter. Even though he did not smoke, he had learned on a job years ago that a lighter is often a great conversation piece. So he always kept a lighter available. The white guy bashed Drew in the head with the object held in his hand. Drew tumbled to the ground.

The disorienting blow was followed by the two men beating

and stomping Drew. Blood rushed from his head. He could feel the life ebbing from him. His body convulsed as they intensified the beating.

"Fucker!" one of them snarled, "This will shut the fucker up!"

The other one was laughing, "Who the hell does this piece of shit think he is?"

Drew was barely conscious, and it was beginning to get difficult to breathe because blood was gushing from his nose. He was so dizzy, and his vision blurred. One of the men urinated profusely on Drew's bleeding body. The other one thought it was a joke and joined suit.

"My God!" Drew thought. He did not even have strength to roll himself away from the stream. Then he saw a light, but was it a light or was it the angel of death? He was too disoriented to know what he was seeing.

"You're going to make it, Drew!"

His mind's eye saw a vision of his grandmother. She was glowing and radiantly smiling. In this strange place between here and there, he could almost touch her. Then just before he passed out, he heard another voice and could hear steps rushing towards him.

"Get the hell away from him!" the familiar voice bellowed. The word "Gino" faintly crossed Drew's swollen lips.

"I will kill you!" A sharp silver object glistened under the street lights. "I will kill you!" The two abusers ran to a nearby parked car and jetted away.

Gino was out of breath by the time he reached him. "Oh my God, Mr. Drew!" He started ripping up his shirt to make strips where he could stop the bleeding. "Oh my God!"

"Gino…ambulance," Drew slurred.

"They don't come down here, Mr. Drew; they don't come down here. But I will take you." Gino was God's angel that night.

He had fortunately been walking back to the boarding house where he lived. He had spotted Drew's car from a distance and saw him in distress.

Drew was taken to the emergency room and admitted to the ICU for severe fractures to his head and face and a few bruised ribs. There would be no justice for Middleton on Monday.

After Drew was released from the ICU, he had a visit from Calvin Row.

"Damn Drew, if you wanted a continuance you could have just filed a motion." Someone needed to lighten up the situation a bit and Calvin really knew how to break the silence.

Drew would have laughed but just trying to cause his face great pain. "Don't know what happened, Calvin."

"Sure you do, Drew; you meddled with the police and the D.A. It's only when you move the ball up the field that you are going to feel the pain. It's called night justice, and it's not in the books. You will learn how things work around here and some choices you will have to make for personal safety."

Drew knew Calvin was telling the truth. But he was also slightly offended, because even though Calvin didn't say it, it was almost as if he had suggested stopping moving the ball up the field. Drew did not comment. He just knew within himself that if the highest price tag he would pay was death, then he had almost crossed that, and if Grandma would be waiting along side Jesus then that would be okay. Besides, blacks had routinely been murdered or had their lives destroyed for years in this racist state for far less than what Drew had done. It would be a badge of honor to join their host.

Drew was released from the hospital one week later. Upon his return, a lot of things had changed. The judge in charge of the prostitution scandal was re-assigned and suddenly promoted to the Court of Appeals. The prosecutor suddenly dropped the case.

Middleton was suddenly cleared of all charges. Drew's attempt to get justice was internally terminated. In a sense, Drew had lost, but, at the same time, it was a victory because corruption had been exposed, and everybody knew that Drew Jones was one to be reckoned with.

Chapter 6

Winter was slowly turning into spring in St. Louis. Drew always looked forward to change and really wished that things could change in the legal system too. It would be wonderful to throw away all of the dead and cold in the system and replace them with something alive and heartwarming. Yes, it was true that some of the things they came up with were bad, but they were still human and deserved some respect. Nothing brought home this calloused indifference more than...

Drew stormed into Calvin Row's office. "They gave him five years probation!" he said, slamming a set of pictures down on Row's desk. "How is he going to survive if he can't carry a weapon to defend himself? He needs witness protection. The Bloods are going to kill him, Row!"

Drew was ranting over Roderick Brown. He had the profile of a typical Public Defender's client—mild mental retardation and a high school dropout. He was charged with unlawful use of a weapon and carrying a concealed weapon.

Roderick was attempting to leave gang life after hearing on the street that a gang was planning on inducting his baby sister into their rival gang. She was the only one he had left. His brother had been killed in a drive-by, his father was already in jail, and his mother was like the living dead. Of course, no one in the police department would consider this because Brown had a pretty bad reputation on the outside. He was trying to get his sister away from the 'hood, so he borrowed a gun and was en route to his uncle's house with his sister when he got pulled over by the police for a missing tail light on his car.

"These pictures are pretty brutal." Row said, reflecting on the size of Brown's testicles. The Boys in Blue gang beat Brown. They kicked him in the testicles until they were half the size of a grapefruit.

"I showed these to Judge Stevenson, and he just shrugged his shoulders. If a judge won't even consider a reprimand for police brutality to this degree, where do I stand? They don't care about anything but their position!"

"You're waking up, Drew."

"I know, but I am not going to become one of them. Justice is not a judge or a jury; it's a fight to pursue what is right at any cost."

"You will not be able to right every wrong, Drew."

"You're not much of a boat rocker, are you?"

"I don't like to look at it that way. I would rather say, I pick my battles wisely and have been around here long enough to know that you can't fight over everything."

"But why did they have to beat him, Row? There are not any notes that he was resisting arrest. He was only stopped for a missing tail light."

"The police do things because they can and they know they will get away with it."

"So is that where it ends?"

"That's for you to decide, Drew. As for me, I just want to keep my job and not set myself up for undue persecution. Just be careful not to burn yourself out," Row advised, "You're needed around here. Why don't you just unwind a little bit? You know the Strassenfest starts today—might be a good time to get away for a while."

"Thanks, but no thanks. I'll just finish up some paperwork."

The Strassenfest was St. Louis' signal for the biggest spring party of the year. It was sheer merry-making madness. Nothing would get done during this time. The office staff was always operating with a skeleton crew. It was welcomed by the court. The Strassenfest was the first of many festivals, and street parties. It was really something like the Midwest version of the Mardi Gras.

It was a time when drunken debauchery was completely acceptable. People's stupor was often covered up by simply joining the Duck Dance contest. This dance made you look drunk even if you weren't. Anyone in the judicial system could act a complete idiot and get away with it. Drew wasn't interested in making himself look like a fool. He'd rather be working.

After a few hours of preparing his next cases and watching the staff slowly drift away as Strassenfest called them outdoors to play, Drew decided to take Row's advice and just ease out of the office. Today of all days, he would not be missed. He decided to take a lesser-used route to the back parking lot. No one hardly ever used this particular exit because you had to walk to the other side of the building to get to it.

As he descended the stairs, he could hear the muffled screams and moans of a woman. He slowly and cautiously proceeded. What he saw was so repulsive that it shocked him speechless. Only God could have sent him down the stairs that day. Three deputy sheriffs had preyed upon a female inmate. One of them, Alexander DuPont, had a reputation of abusing inmates while in their holding cells. It was no surprise that he was part of Judge Stevenson's court where he could fester without reprimand.

It was his white penis that Drew saw shafting the anus of this desperate black woman. The other deputy's white penis was shoved in the woman's mouth, and the third deputy was kicking the woman in the stomach every time her rhythm slowed. DuPont's twisted ecstasy was swiftly interrupted by Drew's death stare.

"STOP!!!" he forcefully snarled.

Their sex party immediately ceased, and DuPont started yelling at the inmate "Stop playing or face going to the hole." They scattered like roaches when the light is turned on.

It took a few minutes for Drew to regain his composure. He wanted to trade his own life for the brutality inflicted upon this victim. Those deputies had broken all protocol. Male deputies weren't even to be around women. But in this system protocol was often exchanged for sick pleasure. The difference was that Drew had never experienced it. He had heard these stories many times, but viewing victimization by trusted officials was debilitating. Each step down those stairs became painful that day.

The sight of blood on those stairs began to stir memories of his own blood as he lay urine-soaked and helpless in the parking lot; it reminded him of Roderick Brown's swollen organs and now of a screaming, helpless woman humiliated and gang-raped. This was the real justice system. Though everybody in the system was not corrupt, too many of them were. They had pledged public safety, but they felt no obligation to those in the doldrums of life. That day Drew vowed that he would never become a part of corruption. He vowed that no amount of social climbing would cause him to lose focus of his divine mission to defend. When he finally arrived home, he took a few pain relievers and sprawled on his bed thinking, *A short day is going to turn into a long night.* He needed comfort, but there was no one around except the voice of his grandmother: "You're going to make it, Drew."

Chapter 7

As the street professionals emerged after dark, Maurita Middleton went about her trade. Suddenly, a dark SUV violently pulled along side her. Two men jumped out of the car. One placed a gun to her head, advised her not to scream and forcefully tossed her onto the backseat floor. She was then tied and gagged. Her eyes were filled with terror. She fought to free herself but to no avail. One of the men said, "It would be too easy to shoot you, Maurita. We've got better things in store."

After driving for what seemed like eternity. The car pulled off on a gravel road. They dragged Middleton from the car into an abandoned warehouse. There was a rope hanging from one of the exposed steel beams and there were three men standing, poised with metal chains and bats. All of a sudden, Middleton did not feel terror anymore. She had moved past that into an acceptance of her fate.

The men tied her feet and hoisted her into the air by the rope. As she was being lifted, she recalled Sister Elena telling her of how Jesus was lifted up on the cross. She rehearsed in her mind the words Sister Elena had spoken, *Father, forgive them for they know not what they do,* then she thought, *Deliver me from evil.* From the corner of her eye, she saw the flick of the silver chain. Her eyes closed.

The next morning Drew arrived at work. He had not gotten much sleep and felt like not coming in. One of the clerks brought a gift-wrapped package to his desk and six long-stemmed roses. "What's going on, Drew?" she smiled.

He gave her a puzzled look. "Really, I don't know what this is all about."

"Just go ahead and pretend you're not the only one who keeps his personal life private," she said laughing.

Drew really did not know what was going on. Just for a moment, he wondered if he had an admirer. When he opened the package it was a box of chocolates and a newspaper that had certain letters highlighted in yellow. The highlighted words simply spelled "Dead End." He got a sick feeling in his stomach that worsened when he read the headline: "Unidentified Woman Bludgeoned." Drew began to shake uncontrollably. He did all he could to hold in the tears.

When the clerk passed by again to see if she could get any more information since the gifts had been opened, she was stunned at the look on his face. "Are you okay, Mr. Jones?"

With lips trembling, he responded, "I need to go down to the coroner. Get the secretary to reschedule any appointments that I have for the day."

"You look ill."

"I'm very ill, and I don't know if I will have time to come back. Tell Mr. Row that Middleton is dead." Drew grabbed his belongings and his "gifts" and left. The entire office was in an uproar when they found out what happened to Middleton.

Drew never liked going to the coroner. It always took a toll on him, but today was so personal to him. He had to pull himself together before he went in to see Mary Rose, the chief medical examiner.

"Has anybody identified the woman found in the building?"

"Drew, I don't know if you want to see this one," said Mary Rose.

"Just take me to the body."

"Listen Drew, this one is bad; we can try to find dental records to determine who she is."

"Let me see the body."

Mary Rose escorted Drew back to the examining room. What he saw caused him to heave. Then he just broke down, "Those bastards!" Middleton had been beaten beyond recognition. Her body was blackened and torn. Her face was so swollen you could not even see where her eyes ended and where her nose and mouth began. Mary Rose pushed a chair for Drew to sit down in. He flopped into the chair, put his head in his hands, and just wept. When he regained himself, he said to Mary Rose, "If she has a tattoo of a cross in her right hand, then this woman is Maurita Middleton."

She acknowledged the tattoo.

Drew gained enough strength to pull himself from the chair. "Can I get you anything, an aspirin—anything?" Mary Rose asked softly.

"This didn't have to happen. She never had much of a chance at life."

Mary Rose handed a few tissues to Drew. "This will get easier for you, even though there are times when this still gets to me. But I do have something to say that I believe will help you to get through this, because I know this is very personal."

"Damn right it's personal."

"She didn't die from the beating. She was already dead before they started in on her. I've never seen anything like it."

Drew took a deep look at Mary Rose. "What?"

"She had been dead about two minutes before the first blow and there were no high levels of adrenaline in her blood."

"She was dead and what was that about her blood?"

"It means she wasn't afraid and that her heart just stopped beating. It was as if the men who did this to her went on a frenzy when they saw that she was already dead."

"Thank you, God!" Drew cried. His mind flashed back to his last conversation with Middleton... *"Are you afraid to die? I'm not."*

"I used to be, but Sister Elena said that God was only a prayer away and that he will listen to us even beyond our last breath. She said after you take your last breath down here, that is when you take your first breath in heaven and you will be with him forever." Drew looked over at Mary Rose, "You will never know what your words meant to me. Middleton is home, and, for the first time in her life, she has peace."

Mary Rose reached over and patted Drew on the shoulder, "I haven't known you very long, but I know you are a good man."

Drew left the coroner's office sad, relieved, yet seething with anger for the hit against Middleton and the fear tactic sent to him. If Middleton could bravely face her torturers, he would in no way be outdone. He was too angry to rest. He had business to take care of. Drew stopped by Sister Elena's on the way back into town. She had already heard about the Jane Doe on the news.

"Sister Elena, you've been working these streets helping people for years; do you know any media sources that can be trusted to spread a leak?"

"You mean the kind that can get the job done and keep their mouth shut."

"Yeah, those are the ones."

"Leave that to me; you just make sure that you steer clear of trouble."

Drew went home.

By the six o'clock news the media was swarming the courthouse over allegations that career and highly respected officer Lee Vincent was involved in human trafficking. They were also hurling accusations that the District Attorney's office was involved in a scandalous cover-up. By the eleven o'clock news, the media was at Drew's apartment seeking a press conference. Everybody was trying to get a question in. Finally, one aggressive reporter blurted out, "Mr. Jones, do you believe that the charges were dropped on Miss Middleton to avoid prosecution?" This was one question Drew would gladly answer because it came straight from the mouth of the D.A.

"In the court system you have to learn that you can't prosecute every thing because some things we pursue only come to a dead end."

"Mr. Jones, Mr. Jones, do you have any further words?" Another reporter interrupted, "Mr. Jones, if Ms. Middleton were alive, do you think she would have eventually dropped the investigation on Vincent?"

"Ms. Middleton was not afraid." Then he looked directly into the camera. "And neither am I. No further questions."

Drew had made his stand in front of the entire city of St. Louis—No fear! The media storm waged for months. It was so severe that Lee Vincent and several of his associates resigned. Drew rejoiced exceedingly when he heard the news. "We did it," he said, gently placing the roses on the grave, "We really did it."

Chapter 8

Eva Richardson was another excellent attorney in the Public Defender's Office. Blake Adams had taken her under his wings right out of law school and helped her to develop herself into a top litigator. She was sensible, detailed and could be quite intimidating just by her looks. Eva was at least five-eleven, slim, blond, and looked German in appearance with striking blue eyes. She always wore conservative dark-colored suits and never had a hair out of place.

So when her personality began to change over a period of months, Blake knew something was not right.

"Eva, how are things going since the divorce?" questioned Blake.

"It's been very difficult, but I've got to move on. Why are you asking me about the divorce, that was eight months ago?"

"You just seemed to be a little distracted lately, and I was just wondering if you were having problems as a result of it because sometimes the stress of a divorce is a delayed reaction."

"I'm not giving him anymore of my time or emotions. Don't worry about me, Blake."

"I've noticed that you have more cases still open than usual, I can shift some things around…"

"I've got it under control, stop worrying about me. I don't

want to talk about it anymore."

Blake nodded his head and walked out of Eva's office. Then he turned back around, reached to the bottom of the stack of files on her desk and took them.

"Blake, don't do that. We don't have enough man power around here to begin with. I can finish those."

He didn't say anything more, he just proceeded out of the office.

Drew had great respect and admiration for Blake Adams and Jeffrey Ellis. He could never repay chief defense attorney Adams for giving him a job, and Jeffrey Ellis, who was the Public Defender's team leader, had become an extreme mentor for him. Drew was being schooled by the finest legal minds in St. Louis: Blake, Jeffrey and Row. There was law and then there was real law. It took real law to survive in this environment, and this is what they taught him. These men were experts on doing the right thing in the midst of corruption.

The law said that a person had the right to competent defense. The real law had exposed lawyers that could not give a shit, being walking violations of the Constitution daily. They only used the Public Defender's Office as a stepping stone to become a "real lawyer." In Drew's eyes, every client had a right to a competent and diligent defense in spite of their ability to pay. To him, there was nothing worse than an unprepared defense attorney who took little care in preparing a case because of lack of monetary motivation or just assuming that the client was guilty anyway, so what's the use? Sometimes Drew wrestled with whose side was the public defender on.

It was times like these when Jeffrey Ellis had been such an inspiration to Drew. He was a true warrior. Jeffrey often gave tips and words of motivation to keep him going. He had taught Drew a lot about dealing in the courtroom. Drew was becoming professionally skilled in closing arguments, making objections even when there was no formal objection to make because of knowledge from this extraordinary team leader who had proven himself to be at the top of the litigation game.

Therefore, it was no amazement when Blake stopped by Drew's office and announced that Jeffrey had just been appointed the City's Chief Attorney by the mayor. The amazement came on the heels of Blake's next words: "You've just been appointed to take Jeff's place, and I know it's not much, but you've been given a three percent raise." Drew was honored and hesitant at the same time.

He wasn't quite sure that he wanted this distinction. Yet, at the same time, he was thankful that Blake had noticed his efforts and that he saw him on the same caliber as Jeffrey—the type of person who would not play games with the "real law." It was as if Blake had officially said *I know you will be there for the clients just like Jeff.* Any apprehensions that Drew had about being elevated this quickly were settled by a thought of what Jeffrey had told him a long time before: "Every man puts his pants on the same way: one leg at a time."

The next time Blake spoke to Drew, it was to discuss his first case in his new position. He was assigned a murder trial; this case was a classic example of legal impotence. Mr. Joseph Clark was arrested and held in the county jail. He had no money, no bail, and no awareness of his legal rights. When Drew was informed about the case, he was appalled that no one had tried the case. Even though according to the file, it had been passed on to several attorneys. Mr. Clark was an old gentle guy locked away on the murder floor of the county jail for two years accused of murdering a teenager. Drew was angry, but, in this case, angry was good. Angry was highly workable.

Drew cleared his desk and went to visit Clark in jail. He was shocked to find a very frail-looking, grey-haired, and nearly toothless man. Everyone on the murder floor had given him the respected name of Pops. Drew wondered what this eighty-three-year-old man could have done to lead him to this hell hole.

He watched as this decrepit gentleman shuffled across the floor to the table where he was sitting. As Clark stepped, Drew noticed that he had passed the old trap door where executions in the early years of the jail were carried out. No one at this age should have to witness such a horrible sight daily, yet, at the same time, he had firsthand knowledge that jails are filled with innocent people who witness the same brutal sight. Technically, he had no right to simply look at Clark and assume his innocence; however, based on the known injustice of the system, he bet he was right about Clark's innocence. He listened intensely as Clark unfolded a tale of lost love, lust, drugs, and perversion. And, as always, the client ended with the mantra: "Do what you can for me, Mr. Jones."

Drew spent all night digging through Mr. Clark's file, uncovering time and time again another mismanaged case and an elderly man who really had no place there suffering. Clark was a distinguished military man. He had served his country well in a time when the army was segregated. He had experienced the ravages of the Klu Klux Klan during his day and had fought to end segregation.

Drew remembered watching Clark's eyes fill with tears as he spoke endearing words about his beloved Estella who had died years ago, how he longed to be with her in the night and desperately needed someone to touch him the way she did. Life showed Clark little mercy, and now he was faced with a murder charge that could destroy the rest of his abbreviated life. Drew knew Clark would rather be dead at this point than alive. But for Drew, he was compelled to change the pending end to this story.

The next day Drew was on the case.

"You know what I read in a file last night?" Drew began as he spoke to Branch, the investigator who had been assigned the case with him.

"What?"

"I read how Anthony Hollis thought more of the dick size of a dead teenager than the life of a distinguished vet. I can't believe a prosecutor would put notes in the file about a man hung as a joke." He shoved the gruesome autopsy pictures across the car seat, "This has got to stop."

Branch looked at the photos without flinching. He had seen hundreds of these morbid shots. "Nobody told you about Hollis before now?"

"Calvin mentioned him."

"I heard he is heavily involved in escort services for the judges and that is how he gets away with so much. And he is Payton Hill's understudy."

"Like father, like son. You know when Middleton died, Hill sent me a newspaper gloating over the fact she was dead."

"She crossed the police and the D.A. It's a wonder she lived as long as she did. You said this guy is eighty-three years old?"

"Yeah."

"And he was doing the girl?"

"To the extent that an eighty-three-year-old man can do anything, but we've got to find somebody to corroborate the story."

They drove to the murder scene, inside Clark's shanty of a house that sat just outside the gang-infested projects. Drew always hated the projects. He considered them a social experiment with black folks that had gone irreparably wrong. *Let's just house all the niggers in low rent buildings, deprive them of adequate schools, remove all infrastructures, deny them access to well-paying jobs, offer them welfare, and see what happens.* It was a breeding ground for daily depravity.

As they opened the door, they could smell the stench of dried urine. The conditions of this shotgun house were deplorable. The only things that were well-preserved were pictures of Estella covering the room. The one that touched Drew's heart the most was the 8x12 photo in that gold frame that had the words "To my true love" scribbled across the bottom half of the picture. The frame faced the bed. He imagined Clark putting himself to sleep every night adoring this once beautiful black woman. She was stunning—long dark hair and deep black eyes that penetrated any onlooker. Her dress revealed a woman of class and style. Drew imagined that Clark's life must have ended the day he buried Estella.

"He must have loved that woman," Branch said as he dug through rubbish looking for clues. "And I bet you anything something about that other woman reminded him of Estella."

"Yep, bet that is how he got into all of this mess." They continued, carefully examining the room for evidence.

After a short while Branch found something. "He ate a lot at The Rib Shack. I've found a lot of old napkins with that name on them."

"Well, you go down to The Rib Shack and see what you can find out, and I'll keep digging around here."

By the time Drew finished scrutinizing the room, he could almost visualize what happened that day. He found money stuffed deep under the mattress and old condoms that had fallen to the floor. As he kept looking, he found a picture of a girl sitting on Clark's lap. *This must be Alexis,* he thought.

She was a long-haired, black beauty, but she was dressed as scantily as a whore. "I can see why he was attracted to her. She does remind you of Estella," he shook his head. "But I know she doesn't have her heart." He also found different types of bracelets and earrings that still had tags on them around the room, almost as if he had given Alexis gifts each time she came by to entertain him.

Branch returned and let Drew know that the two witnesses who were in the police report were down at The Rib Shack. Branch told him about Mario Reid and Germaine Warren, an odd set of friends. From the police report, it appeared that Mario was a smart-ass prick, whereas Germaine was a softer person but mentally challenged. It was probably a situation where Germaine felt empowered as long as he was with Mario. He was more of a yes man.

They quickly drove to The Rib Shack, and Branch pointed them out. Drew approached them and offered to pay for their meal and buy them more food in exchange for some details on Clark. Mario sucked up the opportunity and gladly rattled on about Clark.

"Didn't nobody like the old man; they thought he was crazy," Mario started, "The only reason anybody went around him is because he had drugs and he sold them cheap." Germaine sat nodding his head in agreement. "He was a good cover in the neighborhood; the cops never suspected him of dealing." Drew just sat there listening, suspecting that he was lying because the details of his story were shifting from the documents in the police reports. Mario was the type that would say anything. Drew ordered another round of beers. "Cornbread owed old Joe some money and when he didn't pay him, he stiffed him."

"It was just like that?"

"Yeah man, just like that."

"Either one of you know a girl named Alexis?" Germaine looked over at Mario. "I don't know no Alexis," Mario said hesitantly. Germaine shook his head.

"Thanks for the info, man," Drew said rising up from his seat. "I'm sure we will need to do this again sometime until I wrap up this case. I'll be back." Drew and Branch headed for the car. Mario and Germaine parted ways.

Before they could leave, Germaine ran over to the car. "I know Alexis. She was banging the old man. He just wanted to feel on somebody. She did it to get money to buy water." Branch's head lifted at the slang term for PCP and looked at Drew. "He didn't know that she was fucking Cornbread too."

"So Cornbread confronted Mr. Clark when he didn't pay for servicing that day?"

"No he did pay. I saw the money. Alexis just told Cornbread that he didn't pay so that she could keep the money."

Just for a moment, Drew's mind went back to his brother DeMarcus. A hell-bent woman is as deadly as arsenic.

"Cornbread needed a fix. So he kicked in Clark's door and beat the hell out of him and told him if he did not have his money when he came back he would kill him."

Drew pressed him a little more, "So he came back..." "Yeah, we all heard the gunshot. We knew Cornbread was dead. Me and Mario ran over to Clark's house. Cornbread's chest was blown open, and he was lying in blood. Mr. Clark was sitting on the bed crying like a baby. We ran out of there before the police came."

"When did the police catch up with you guys?"

"They found us the next day, and Mario told them the story he told you because he always wanted a piece of Alexis, but was scared of Cornbread. Now with him dead, he could do what he wanted."

When Drew got in the car, he just shook his head. It took a bag of ribs, six quarts of beer, and a jury that deliberated fifteen minutes to acquit Mr. Clark on grounds of self defense. A botched investigation had cost a desperate, lonely old man two years on the murder floor at the county jail. Upon hearing the jury's verdict, a teary-eyed Mr. Clark squeezed Drew's hand. "God bless you, son." Those words are what Drew lived for.

Chapter 9

Mario was furious when he found out that Germaine had been the star witness for Drew at Mr. Clark's trial. He confronted Germaine as he left the courthouse. His foul language spewed like an uncapped cesspool. "What the fuck did you do that for man?" he said pushing Germaine.

"I did it for old man Clark…you always lying about stuff, but this time…"

"But 'this time,' what? Clark's been in jail for two years. Nobody was even thinking about him. What the hell is he to you anyway?"

Germaine kept trying to walk briskly, pushing his way around Mario.

"You ain't going to answer me! You made the cops look stupid now they are going to be all over us!"

Germaine kept walking. Mario grabbed him and threw him up against the wall. Germaine mumbled, "Look man, I've been eaten up every time I thought about seeing that old man handcuffed for some damn shit Alexis did. Mr. Clark ain't never hurt anybody. I should have made it right the first time…"

"Fucker, you're getting soft, and down here getting soft ain't nothing but trouble." Mario got within a breath of Germaine. "Do some dumb ass shit like that again and I will kill you!" he said slinging him to the ground.

Germaine knew that Mario was fully capable of carrying out that threat and made it his business to stay away from him for the next few months, but Mario was seething. He had a fierce reputation on the street, and it did not leave room for being ratted out. The best place for a snitch was dead. But even Mario had one uncorrupted spot. He had known Germaine too long and decided not to have his blood on his hands. That was until Christmas Eve was interrupted by a cold-blooded murder.

Officers swarmed Meyer Park Plaza. All Points Bulletins were placed for anything that could be possibly considered a suspect. One of their own had fallen. His crimson blood pierced the brilliant white snow. Police Sergeant Don Henderson was dead with a gunshot wound to the neck. Henderson was alone that night and was said to be patrolling the parking lot. Nothing gets St. Louis police in a tizzy like losing one of their own. Someone would pay. The patrols were nonstop. Every known homeless man or alleged street thug was rounded up, brought down to the county jail, and beaten if the cops thought he might be remotely related to the incident. The St. Louis police had a way of suspending "the law" when they were on a witch hunt for a cop killer.

It didn't take them very long to arrest Mario Reid. He was always a suspect. They beat him severely. After getting knocked around for a while, he decided to do what was so common to him and lie. But this lie had a motive. Even in his worst state of affairs, his mind plotted evil. He just tearfully planted another story in the minds of the police. He was not the killer, but he knew who was. He said it was Germaine Warren. Perhaps they would beat him to death so that he would not have to. To him this was karma.

Germaine was a good guy. He just happened to associate with some very bad characters. It might have been a matter of survival, knowing that he needed street protection. Mario had become a big brother to him in a negative way. He never would have expected that crossing Mario would have murderous implications. He was sitting at home on Christmas Eve wrapping gifts with his family when swarms of police officers, SWAT teams, and homicide detectives surrounded and overtook his home.

Germaine was completely bewildered. He pleaded with the police to hear him. But they just dragged him from his home and battered him through the night. He was not allowed an attorney or explained his Miranda rights. The boys wanted a confession, and they knew how to get one. They played games with his mind. They deprived him of food and water. And in addition to the merciless beatings, they tortured him by putting a gun in his mouth, threatening to blow his brains out.

After the torture-induced confession, the police blanketed the news of how they found the crazed cop-killing nigger. The D.A. Payton Hill planned to take this case to death. No one kills a cop and lives to tell about it. The prevailing view was if you confessed, you did it, despite how the confession was obtained.

Drew had intended to have a very peaceful Christmas Eve. He had been out with a few old friends, stopped by a local Chinese hole-in-the-wall for his favorite take-out, and decided to end the day watching *It's a Wonderful Life*. Somehow he just really loved identifying with George Bailey who worked so hard to help people despite all the opposition that life brings. It reminded him that life is worth living.

Just as he was about to pop the DVD in, he saw a picture of Germaine's face on the local news. *Oh my God*, he thought, *what happened now?* He reached over to the remote and frantically turned up the volume. The newscaster announced, "The St. Louis police are holding suspect Germaine Warren for the murder of Police Sergeant Don Henderson. He is being held without bail in the county jail. According to a witness, Warren had told him that he shot Henderson after the officer startled him during an attempted car theft. We will keep you updated on further developments with this case."

"No!" Drew winced. He turned around, put his coat back on and headed for the county jail.

Drew watched Germaine drag his battered body across the trap door on the murder floor; he couldn't help but to wonder if Germaine wished that he were actually falling through that door instead of facing a cop-killing trial. As he approached, Drew could smell the stench of human waste on his body, evidenced by brown stains on his pants. They had degraded this man and were not even merciful enough to give him a bar of soap after his unwarranted abuse.

Tears stained Germaine's swollen face. "I didn't do it, Mr. Jones. Mario…"

"I know Germaine. I just hate that I am a part of you being here."

"It wasn't you, Mr. Jones. I had to stand up for Mr. Clark. He was too old to die in jail. Mario was mad enough to kill me when I did it. This is just his way of getting revenge."

Drew took out his digital camera from his coat pocket and began taking pictures of Germaine's injuries, "We're going to get you out of here."

"Mr. Jones, I already told them I did not want anyone else to help me but you."

On the inside, he was thinking to himself, "*What am I saying?*" He knew his experience with murder trials was limited, but, at the same time, he knew he could not stand this type of injustice. He was almost killed before for crossing the system, and he knew taking on this case was like inviting a noose on himself. It was times like these that all the messages of courage from his upbringing would begin to speak to him. Some things you just have to do because it's right to do…

"You're going up against Payton Hill on this one," Blake Adams said as he passed the file to Drew. Everyone knew that Payton Hill was Mr. Death Sentence himself. He was an expert at sending inmates to their demise. "You can't be intimidated by that either. One thing you will have to learn is that every attorney, no matter how good he is, has an Achilles heel. You already know this is a high-profile case; just find the heel."

Drew was not looking forward to this. Public favor was already been drawn to Don Henderson. How would they find an impartial jury? Every news media was blasting the story. Images of Henderson's bereaved wife were all playing into the drama.

Drew recalled the last newscast: "We're seeking the death penalty on this one," Payton Hill said as he stood next to a weeping Amanda Henderson.

"My husband was on his way home for Christmas. How could anyone do this to him?" she sobbed.

Amanda's mind betrayed her. *Get your hands off of me, Don!* She relived the pain of her body crashing against the wall in their bedroom.

"We will protect our police officers at all cost and will rid our communities of these dope-crazed individuals. You can be assured of that. Warren has already confessed to the killing. It is our job to make sure that justice is served."

Drew wanted to vomit.

He knew what he had to do: look at Hill's footprints and find a spot on his heel. After a little digging, Drew found out that Jeffrey Ellis was one of the few attorneys who had ever won a case against Mr. Death Sentence. In order not to smear his new position as city attorney by being drawn into this case, Drew just decided to show up at one of Jeffrey's known hang-outs and hope he would be there at happy hour. It was a good move. They had a drink together, and Jeffrey gave him what he needed. "Read every inch of the police reports and use every detail to your advantage. It has been my experience that many attorney's fail to carefully read the police reports. I have found that the main things they overlook or fail to follow up on are gold for me. It's always in the police reports. Just don't lose hope and give up." The two quickly parted. Drew was so grateful of his association with Ellis.

Drew got busy and filed all the standard motions to produce discovery. He wanted everything created on this case, and all his requests were in bold print. That even got Hill's attention; he personally called Drew. "I've heard about you, but I think you are over your head with this one." He thought it was a joke, but he delivered three banker boxes of police reports to the Public Defender's Office the next day.

Chapter 10

The phone was ringing in Eva Richardson's apartment as she entered the door. She rushed over to the phone because she was anticipating a call.

"Hello."

"You have a collect call from Mr. Jacob Black. Will you accept the charge?"

"Yes." The operator got off the line.

"Hi baby," said Black.

"Hi."

"I miss you."

"I miss you too," Eva felt her heart racing.

This was an odd interracial relationship. They had met under the most unusual circumstance. They were complete opposite. Black's influence on Richardson was almost as if she was under a spell. Her mind flashed back to the last time she had seen him. She was lying on the floor. Her thong had been removed, and Black was grinding her climatically. As the thought crossed her mind, she fanned herself while still visualizing herself desperately clutching his dark muscular six-foot body.

"Will you have any time to see me tomorrow?"

"I will try," she said, "but I did get your package."

"That's good."

"What do you want to eat, if I can make it?"

"Why don't you stop by that Muslim fish shop on 23rd Street and bring me a three-piece dinner."

"Okay. I will see you tomorrow," she slowly put the receiver down.

As Payton Hill and Amanda Henderson were making their rounds for public support on every local station and national morning shows, Drew was sitting at his desk scrutinizing every line of the reports and listening to police interrogation tapes. Hill's approach had two purposes. He was up for re-election and the more public exposure the better. Second, by exploiting a high profile case finding a jury that would be more willing to execute would be easier, the more they could paint a negative picture on the news. Drew, on the other hand, had been unfolding quite an interesting scandal from his research.

When Amanda got home that afternoon, she quickly pulled her shoes off aching feet and flopped down on the living room sofa. The house was very quite, and it would be a few hours before the children got home from school. Amanda hated the silence. Even though she could interrupt it with the sound of the television, it was not enough to dull the painful memories in her head.

She picked up the remote from the coffee table and began channel surfing. The Lifetime Channel caught her attention. Her eyes were fixed on a terrified female character running through a dark parking lot being chased by a man with a knife. Her mind shifted to her running from Don after they had gotten into a fierce argument on a hunting trip. He tackled her, and she fell to the ground, landing on a pile of fallen leaves.

"When I tell you to stay out certain areas of my life you don't go and hire an investigator! I am a damn cop; you didn't think I would find out! If you wanted to know who I am sleeping with and what else I am doing why didn't you just ask me?"

Amanda spit in Don's face. He gave her a hard slap. "*I don't need you anymore, you bastard. Two can play that game.*"

"*Bring a man around and I will kill both of you... Who's going to take care of you like I do? You get everything that you want. You haven't worked in ten years.*"

"*I'd rather have the opportunity to cash in the policy.*" She felt Don's hands wrap around her neck. *You're threatening to have me killed?* Amanda remembered how hopeless she felt as she tried to struggle loose from his grip. Before she passed out, he released her and walked back to the truck. She lay there gasping for air...

Drew went out to lunch with Calvin Row. They went to a local Red Lobster and were eating their lunch when they happened to see Blake Adams there. He was having lunch with a stunning-looking red-haired. They waved to Blake.

"Who's that?" Drew asked.

"They tell me that is the end of the bachelor road," Calvin replied.

"You're kidding."

"No, that one is going to tame the tiger."

Blake Adams had a reputation of being an outstanding lawyer and one that would defend his attorney's until the end. But he also had a reputation of being a ladies man, and no one until this point seemed to be able to tie him down. Marriage had always taken a back seat to his career.

Blake was a handsome man and had aged gracefully at fifty-two. He was five-six with silver and pepper hair. He kept in shape and weighed about 170 pounds. He almost looked Mediterranean. His skin was tanned and his deep blue eyes looked like pools of turquoise water. It was rumored that he had gone through more relationships than hot knives have gone through butter.

"Her name is Arlene Clydesdale. I heard he was planning on getting engaged."

"He does seem happy lately."

"Yeah, happy enough to pass off some of Eva Richardson's cases."

"Oh goodness, you got some of those too?"

"Uh-huh. But she doesn't seem to be doing well lately. She is too distracted, and that is normally not her," Calvin said, "She got divorced a few months ago, and that might have something to do with it."

"I've sat in on some of her cases, and she is good."

"I know. That's why it is hard to see her in a daze."

"Has anybody tried to talk with her to see if she needs anything?"

"It really doesn't work like that around there. People might care, but they don't really get involved. Blake probably has said something. Besides, Richardson is pretty much a loner. She carries herself very professionally and never gotten involved in office junk."

Blake got ready to leave the restaurant. He and Arlene stopped by Drew's table.

"Arlene wanted to meet the guy that is going to take on Payton Hill in the Henderson case," Blake said smiling. "Drew, this is Arlene Clydesdale."

Drew reached out and shook her hand and smiled.

"You already know Calvin."

"Yes," she said, "It's nice seeing you again. I wish the case was in my court. I hear it is going to quite an interesting trial from all the media involvement."

"I didn't know you were a judge," Calvin said.

"Yep, been on the bench fifteen years, but I don't work in your division. I am a judge in personal injury."

Drew looked at Arlene's hand and could not help to notice the four rows of diamonds in one band on her ring finger. *Blake spent a pretty penny*, he thought.

"How is your information shaping up on the case?" Blake asked.

"It's looking well. There are a lot of unbelievable elements in the case, but I think they are going to do well enough to get Germaine out of harm's way."

"Well, I will be attending the entire event. This is going to be a good and, I believe, a controversial trial."

"I appreciate your support, Blake."

He nodded and then escorted Arlene out of the restaurant.

"Did you notice the ring?" Calvin asked.

"Who could have missed that one?"

They both laughed and continued their lunch.

When they returned from lunch, the docket controller quickly assigned the death penalty case. The court loved being sensationalized over the Henderson case. Drew left the office about six thirty that evening. He was surprised to see a note on his desk from Eva Richardson. The note read:

"I know that Blake gave you, Calvin, and Robert some of my assignments. As the new kid on the block I hate to be a burden to you. At least let me buy you a cup of coffee and a donut." Tucked in the note was a ten dollars certificate to Star Bucks.

"Wow," Drew thought. "Who would have thought this would happen. She hardly says anything to me. There must be something sensitive under all of that conservatism."

By 7 o clock Eva had made her way into the county jail. The routine had been the same for quite a few months. She went through the metal detectors; put all her bags and packages on the conveyor. No one ever expected that the care packages of toiletries contained crack in the bottom of the bottles of baby powder that Eva would bring. Then she would be escorted by Sheriff Michaels to the visiting room.

He was always eager to take her packages (he knew about the drugs), but they would never make it to the visiting room. Eva would always stop by the staff's restroom on her way up to the visiting room. That was really as far as she had to go, because there would always be someone waiting for her in the lounge area of the rest room. Sheriff Michaels would see to that. He would also see to it that once Eva entered, the door was locked and an "out of service" sign would be posted to the door. She knew he would always be back in forty minutes.

Jacob Black was sitting on a bench the size of a window seat when she came in. He stood to great her, and they exchanged a long embrace then sat back down.

"Michaels will bring you the fish dinner later, okay."

"That's fine, but I am just glad you came."

"Are you glad I came or are you glad to see me?"

"Eva, you know we don't have a lot of time what's this all about?"

"People are beginning to notice me at work. They know something is not right, and I just don't think I can take the pressure of bringing the packages anymore. Now they are taking my assignments and giving them to other people at work because I am so distracted."

Jacob didn't say anything. He just started caressing Eva's body. Today she wore nothing but a sweat suit under her coat. He took one hand, put it under her shirt, and began fondling her large breasts.

"Are you listening to me Jacob?"

He proceeded to kiss her neck, and she could feel her body responding.

"I love you, baby, don't stop coming now."

She had lived eight years in a practically loveless marriage, the way Jacob paid attention to her physically and his constantly expressing how much he missed her and loved her kept her coming back. Eva was an emotionally starved woman until Jacob entered her life.

"You love me, Jacob?"

"Hell yes...take off your shirt."

"I really need to know if you love me. I couldn't live if I thought this was all a fantasy for me."

He grabbed her shirt and pulled it over her head. His mouth consumed her swollen nipples. "I love you, Eva," he kissed her all over into submission. They ended up back on the floor again. They were making love on top of her coat, which was lying on the floor.

Eva got up quickly and dressed herself the moment it was over.

"Jacob, I've never told you 'thank you' for saving me."

"Eva, you've never told me what happened..."

"Please don't ask now. One day I will be able to talk about it, but not today. I love you, Jacob, and I will be back soon."

They gave each other one last hard kiss. Shortly after, they heard two thumps on the door and knew that was Michaels telling them their time was up. They unlocked the door from within. She left first, and then several minutes later Michaels came back, gave him few minutes to eat, and then escorted him back to his cell.

Eva got into her black SAAB and drove home. Her mind flowed in and out with thoughts about Jacob and her ex-husband David. *"You know I am guilty don't you."*

"I hate to say this, Mr. Black, but you are a piece of shit for what you did."

"Then why are you taking my case?" "Because that is my job, and I am damn good at what I do."
"I just thought you liked me."
"You are sick."

Eva's mind began to rehearse all the flirtations Jacob had expressed during their many meeting together. A part of her wanted to reject his advances, but there was also a part of her that got heated. It was little things like brushing up against her when they left a meeting, or touching her leg under a table where they sat, or making kissing gestures with his lips.

When she looked across the table at him, she could not deny that he was good-looking man. He was tall, muscular, and had a slick bald head, and his face was accented by a mustache. His eyes seemed to penetrate her. They looked like a tiger's eye stone. He had perfect teeth. As evil as he was, he always managed to say something, flash his smile, and get a reaction from her.

Under normal circumstances Eva's ability to be cold and emotionless would have thwarted any attempts of flirtation, but her husband David had done something that left her emotionally wide open, if only to get back at him. Her mind flashed to another meeting with Jacob.

"Why do you always dress like a stiff bitch?" "Mr. Black, I am trying to keep you from getting executed. I don't have time for this. You need to cooperate with me."

"You look like you're pent up. I just can't figure out if you are pent up because you are angry or whether you are a sexually frustrated woman."

"Okay, that's it I am calling a guard to get you out of here."

"If you need a real man instead of that puppy you have at home I can fix that." A guard came in and escorted him out of the room.

Her mind shifted once again to several months later, but this time tears began streaming down her face. She recalled the first day that she found out David, a college professor, was having an affair with one of his students. She felt the devastation of not feeling good enough to keep him attracted. She remembered all the months she said nothing to him about it because her mother had always told her that you can expect a man to cheat but that does not have to end your relationship: *"I put up with your father's mess and it kept our family together. Sometimes you make sacrifices because you know it's only a fling."*

Eva longed to be as strong as her mother so she put up with a lot of David's cheating. They were just what her mother said—just flings. But this one with Katherine did not end. She had put up with it for three years and had gotten fed up with it. So she went to his office one day to finally confront him…

"I told you not to come up here."

"David, I've just got to get some things out. You're not treating me right."

"You need to leave."

"I'm not leaving this time. You better listen to me. I am tired of putting up with you and your whore. I sacrificed my whole life, helped you get your damn PhD for us to have a better life. Not for you to give your life away to some tramp that is half your age."

"She is not a tramp or a whore, and I don't care what you think. You were always to busy to be with me so…"

"Don't blame this on me, David. Somebody had to make the money while you were in school…"

Just then the door opened. Katherine walked in. David covered his face with his hands. Eva turned, and her jaw dropped open. She braced herself against David's desk.

"She's pregnant…" Eva said emotionally reeling. Katherine looked to be a few months pregnant.

"I'm sorry. I didn't know she was in here, David. I'm so sorry."

Eva took her handbag and started slamming it on David's head. Then she dropped the bag and just started beating him.

David did his best to restrain her, but between her weeping and kicking it was too much for him to handle.

"Eva, get control of yourself. I couldn't tell you this. That is why I told you not to come up here!"

"You no good son of a bitch! All those years I wanted children, and you said we need to get our careers in order. Then we got our careers in order, you said maybe later. I begged you for a child… David how could you!!!"

Katherine was about to walk out the room.

"Don't leave. I am leaving, and you can have this…" Eva snatched her wedding bands off and threw them at Katherine, then stormed out the door.

By this time Eva was crying so hard that she could barely see the road in front of her. She still had another twenty-minute drive to get home. This was going to be a long ride. Another memory flashed into her mind.

Eva knew the system well. She knew whom she could trust to do something legal or illegal. But the pain David caused sent her into the dark side. After driving around for hours after she had the encounter with David and Katherine she stopped by the county jail.

"I need to see Sheriff Michaels," she told one of the clerks.

Michaels came out to greet Eva. "Hi Mrs. Richardson, what brings you by here so late this evening. I thought they would give you a short break after Jacob Black's sentencing."

"We don't get breaks in the Public Defender's Office. The more efficiently you work, the more you are rewarded with more cases."

"I need a private audience with Mr. Black."

"Okay, I will try to get you an area that is private enough to talk."

"No, I need his services for about an hour in a private area."

"You want to be alone with Mr. Black?"

"Right now and you owe me for that traffic ticket that got lost."

"I'll arrange it, but now if you come back you will owe me."

"What do you want?"

"Anything white and sellable."

"If I am back, where do I get it?"

"At Chin's Laundry. Just tell them I sent you."

Eva felt her heart racing the whole time, but she was so angry with David that she just wanted to do something that would cause him pain. She would surely tell him what she had done. How he was responsible for driving her to this edge.

"I am going to put an 'out of order' sign on the staff restroom. You can go in there and wait. I'll bring him down and will lock you two in the room for one hour and that's it. This is not like you, but if this is what you want I'll do it. Are you sure?"

"It's none of your business. Let's just make this transaction."

Eva walked off and went to the staff restroom. Jacob was brought down about ten minutes later. Michaels did not tell him what was going on. He thought Michaels needed him to do some kind of inside job for him. When he pushed the door open, Eva was standing there nude. Every hair on his body stood up, and he could feel his body responding to her beauty.

"You said I was an angry and sexually frustrated woman and you could fix it. Let's see what you've got behind that foul mouth of yours."

Jacob was so shocked he did not know what to say. He thought he was dreaming and literally slapped himself.

"What the hell are you doing, lady?"

She walked over to him and got in his face and hissed.

"So used to taking what you want, you don't know what to do when someone gives it to you. Am I too much for you, bad boy? Are you just a bunch of talk?"

Jacob grabbed the back of her head and forced her head forward until their lips met. She unloosed his pants, and they dropped to the floor. Jacob pushed her back long enough to take his shirt off. The rest of their actions were almost animal on the floor. Eva unleashed every ounce of her anger on Jacob. She riddled his body with bite marks and clawed his back, drawing blood. He bruised her body with passion marks from the neck down. His off-balanced mind took pleasure in the pain she was inflicting on him.

"Is that all you've got," she whispered, "Harder."

He plunged into her until she bit him hard enough for him to know that it was over. That was the best she could do since she could not scream. He released himself and went limp. When he gained enough strength, he said, "Lady, where has your husband been or have you killed him?"

"Don't you ever mention my husband to me."

Eva dressed herself and then tossed Jacob his clothes. He quickly put them on.

"So that's it, did I fix your problem?"

"Don't pride yourself."

Jacob backed Eva into the corner of the room.

"I'm not your boy toy."

"Don't like not being in control do you?"

"I'm in control, baby."

"We will see."

Eva grabbed her bag, unlocked the door, and walked out. Jacob sat down, confused, not knowing what really just happened. He waited until Michaels came for him.

The only problem with this situation was that Eva and Jacob realized they had chemistry that evening. Neither of them had been involved that intensely before, and it scared both of them. Eva kept coming back, and it wasn't long before raw passion budded into an unusual love that kept them glued together. Eva's emotions were so scrambled that she began to unravel at work.

"If I had only met you earlier in my life, I would not be here in this jail," said Jacob, *"It's amazing what real love and a good woman will do."* Eva's eye's welled with tears at that thought. She had learned quite a bit about Jacob, and there were some very serious issues that sent him into a deranged life. She understood how pain can trigger the worst in people.

Eva pulled into her driveway. She was happy to have been with Jacob, but totally disgusted because she knew the relationship could not go anywhere. He had life in prison without parole for what he had done. But for now, he was meeting a need that David had crushed. Jacob satisfied her deeply and made her feel worth something. She never had intended for it to go this far.

Several weeks had passed. It seemed that every news channel in St. Louis and many national affiliates were still inhaling every ounce of the Henderson drama. Drew even decided to get in on some of it. He at least had to look the part of a smooth operator. He made sure to have at least five suits for the trial—two of them just purchased. He was as polished as a high-class store mannequin on a bargain-basement budget.

The jury selection took another two weeks with death qualification questions. The process took so long because in a trial like this the jurist would have to say that he or she would be willing to sentence the defendant to death in order to be qualified to serve. People against the death sentence would be kicked out of the process. The final jury was composed of nine whites and three blacks. The ratio of men to women was equal. Drew fully understood the nature of the game, and knew he would have to paint a picture of Germaine as a mistreated man. He knew that it would be harder to kill Germaine if the jury saw him as a person and not a cop killer.

Payton Hill had already done an excellent job doing that. A dope-crazed nigger was always a threat to white America. Those words would forever send a chilling message with roots back to the days of lynch mobs said to be defending the honor of white women that had been allegedly violated. His selection of words had set the grounds for execution well.

Opening statements began. The courtroom was packed. The reporters and all the attorneys from both the Prosecutor's and the Public Defender's Offices came out to view the spectacle. This was more than a police murder trial. It was a show down between a young black upstart who had already bucked the system and one of their finest legal minds. The bets were in again, and it was apparent whose side the majority stood for. No one wanted to see Hill go down—the little young Negro needed a lesson.

Payton Hill started his opening statement like a surgeon preparing to cut on the dotted line. The patient was Germaine Warren, and Hill didn't intend to use an anesthetic. Drew sat in the opposing corner with Blake Adams encouraging him all the way. Amanda Henderson was dressed in mourning clothes, mascara dripping, and looking like she needed smelling salts to stay coherent. The media was eating it up and broadcasting live. There could be no mistakes.

"What could be more sinister than slaying a police officer?" Hill began, "The autopsy report noted that he suffered for at least eight minutes before his life ebbed away—despite the best efforts of the paramedics to save him. I wonder what Mr. Warren was doing during that time as Officer Henderson lay wounded and convulsing in the cold snow. We must stop all the dope-crazed killings!"

"Objection, Your Honor; citing relevance and argumentative."

"Overruled, Mr. Jones. Hill, keep all comments relevant," ordered Judge Roberts.

Hill continued. "On Christmas Eve, when most of us were enjoying our families and looking forward to the wonder of our children, Mrs. Henderson was on her way to the morgue." He pointed to the grief stricken wife. "The love of her life taken away, leaving her with awesome burden of raising her three children alone. Should this have happened? An officer was doing his job protecting the community! Should this have happened? I say to you NO. Do the right thing while listening to the evidence." Hill sat down.

Drew began his opening statement like a skilled potter. He would mold the hearts of the jury to fit his side of the story. "Are we not innocent until proven guilty in our great country? Yet Mr. Warren was proven guilty before trial by our finest police officers. Mr. Warren is a gentle man."

"Objection!" Hill countered. "Sustained." said Judge Roberts. "Let me rephrase that; he has no record of violence and has only been arrested once for suspicion of marijuana possession—a common drug that many of you can probably relate to in your own lives."

"Objection, this is personalization of the jury, Your Honor!"

"Mr. Jones, stick to the matters at hand."

Drew continued, "I tell you anyone would confess if they were beaten within inches of their own life and left to wallow in their own defecation as part of the punishment!" He could feel the discomfort of the audience, and murmurs went through the crowd. He pointed at Germaine. "There were lots of people that the police could have questioned, but they did not. Instead they took the word of a very well-known felon and built a cause around that. Records indicate that Mr. Warren has a near mentally challenged I.Q. He's simply not capable of this heinous crime. This is clearly a rush to justice. Do your duty and listen closely to the evidence."

Hill began to call his witnesses. Drew was impressed. He was a marksman at prosecution. He touched every base and seemed to have made his case with every witness. He had elevated himself in the eyes of the jury, and they were fixed on him as one mesmerized by the beauty of a hot air balloon.

Payton Hill called Mario Reid to the witness stand.

"Mr. Reid, can you tell the jury what your relationship to the defendant is?"

"We have known each other for ten years."

"Was the defendant with you on the night of December 24 at 9:00 PM?"

"Yes."

"Where were you and the defendant that night?"

"We were in Myer Plaza in the parking lot."

"Can you please tell the jury what you were doing at the time?"

"We were going around the parking lot trying to find cars that were easy to get in to."

"So you were attempting to steal cars?"

"No we were only trying to break in to them to find anything valuable that we could sell, and we knew lots of people leave gifts in the cars on holiday's that would be expensive."

"Why were you trying to find items you could sell?"

"Cause we were out of drugs."

"Objection. Speculation and materiality," Drew stated.

"Sustained."

"Let me rephrase that question. Was there a motive for the thefts?"

"Germaine told me that we needed some crack and that breaking in cars on Christmas Eve could get us enough money to last a while."

"What happened next?"

"We broke into several cars and stole stuff like radios and small packages."

"At what point did you encounter Officer Henderson?"

"After we had broken into about five cars."

"Where were you?"

"In the back of the Sears parking lot."

"What happened next?"

"Germaine had a gun, and he was hitting the butt of the gun on the glass of the car trying to bust the window. The window finally shattered, and Germaine opened the door to the car. We both got in the car. I started going through the glove compartment, and he started unwiring the radio. That's when we heard Officer Henderson."

"Describe how you heard Officer Henderson."

"First I heard someone running, then I heard someone say, 'Police get away from the vehicle.' But by that time, he was already on Germaine's side of the car."

"Then what happened?"

"Officer Henderson grabbed Germaine's legs and started pulling him from the vehicle. Germaine was struggling to kick him loose, and then he grabbed his gun and shot Henderson in the neck. Officer Henderson fell backwards hitting the ground. Me and Germaine crawled out to the other side of the car and ran."

"No further questions."

Drew got up to cross-examine the witness.

"Mr. Reid, can you describe the car that you were in at the time Officer Henderson found you?"

"I think it was a black Trail Blazer."

"Why do just think it was a black Trail Blazer? Wouldn't you know?"

"We broke into a lot of cars that night; it's hard to remember which one it was."

"Did you break in more than five cars as you stated earlier?"
"No."
"Then I don't think it would be difficult to remember the last car out of only five."
"Objection. He's badgering the witness, Your Honor."
"Overruled."
"Your Honor, I would like Defense exhibit one passed to the jury."
"Objection."
"Overruled."
Drew passed the pictures to the jury. Then he passed the pictures to Mario.
"Mr. Reid, can you describe to the jury what you see in that picture?"
"A large parking lot of cars."
"Is there snow on the ground?"
"Yes."
"Is there lots of snow or a little snow?"
"Lots of snow."
"Is there snow all around the cars that you see in the parking lot?"
"Yes."
"Do you see any cars in that photo that you recognize?"
"There is a black car near the back of the parking lot."
"Are there more than one black car in the parking lot?"
"Yes."
"Would you look to the right of the exhibit and tell me what you see?"
"A brown Escalade."
"Is there snow around the Escalade?"
"Yes."
"Is the snow smooth like it has just fallen?"

"No."
"What does the snow look like?"
"It has tire marks in it."
"Anything besides tire prints."
"No."
"Are you certain?"
"Yes."
"Would you please examine the exhibit again and tell me what do you see in the snow near the back of the Escalade?"
"Foot prints."
"Do you see any more foot prints?"
"No."
"Is there a car next to the Escalade?"
"Yes."
"When you saw Officer Henderson, can you tell me about how tall he was?"
"A little over six feet tall."
"You stated that Mr. Warren shot him in the neck and he fell backwards hitting the ground."
"Yes."
"But isn't there a car on the side of the Escalade?"
"I just knew he had to hit the ground because I was running."
"That was not your testimony, and you are under oath. No further questions."

Payton Hill called his next witness, Medical Examiner Pruitt.

"Dr. Pruitt, I show you the State's exhibit number one, which is your autopsy photo of Officer Henderson. Can you identify it?

"Objections to the photos because they are too gruesome, hideous, and not probative of any relevant issue."

"Overruled Mr. Jones. He only asked the witness to identify the exhibit."

"They are the autopsy photos I took of Officer Henderson

showing the damage he sustained in the gunshot wound."

"Your Honor, I would like to pass the photos to the jury."

"Objections, due to the same grounds stated before."

"Sustained. There is no need for the jury to see those photos due to their ability to inflame the jurist."

"Can you tell us which path the bullet traveled causing death to Officer Henderson."

"It entered the body from the right side of the neck and traveled downward severing the jugular vein. The fragments entered his right lung and kidneys. The cause of death was sanquination or the loss of blood."

"Do you mean he suffocated in his own blood?"

"That is correct and or loss of blood to his vital organs."

"What type of weapon killed Officer Henderson?"

"It was a .38 caliber pistol."

"Did ballistics from weapon that was later found registered to Mr. Warren match the bullet in the deceased?"

"The results are inconclusive due to the amount of fragmentation of the bullet, but it was the same type of weapon."

"No further questions."

Drew cross-examined Dr. Pruitt.

"Dr. Pruitt, your testimony is that the bullet traveled in a downward direction; is that correct?"

"Yes."

"Did you examine the decedent, Officer Henderson, in total?"

"Yes."

"Did you examine his knees for bruises or blood around the knee tissue?"

"Yes."

"Was there any bruising and or pooling of blood in the knee tissue?"

"But this could have taken place anywhere?"
"Please respond yes or no."
"Yes."
"Could they have occurred if he were in a kneeling position?"
"Yes, but we don't have any evidence that he was kneeling."
"Let's let the judge and jury determine the evidence please. No further questions."

Judge Roberts called for a recess of the trial until 10:00 AM the next day.

At the close of the business day, Eva Richardson went home quickly. It was her new routine since she had gotten involved with Jacob. He would always try to call between 6:30 and 7:30 PM. Her response was always the same, a rush of adrenaline, a forbidden excitement that she could not explain. Their conversations would range from normal to bizarre with neither of them wanting to end a call. The phone finally rang at 7:00 PM, and she accepted the charge.

"How's my girl?"
"Good."
"Can you come see me this week?"
"I'm thinking it won't be before Tuesday of next week."
"You don't have to bring a package. I've still got plenty of soap and stuff."
"Jacob, you always use up the stuff I bring. What, they are not letting you use it?"
"No, I'm still using your stuff, but I know with you working and everything you have to go through so much to get just the right things for me and I thought I'd give you a break for a while. Trust me, there's no shortage of soap and stuff around here. I'll just borrow what I need. I just don't want you under any pressure. You were pretty stressed out the other day."

Eva sat there crying, because the worst part of the ordeal in her mind was bringing drugs into the prison and he just told her to stop doing it.

"What about that guy you used to share with because no one ever sent him anything. He seemed to like getting stuff."

"Don't worry about him. I know you've gotten to know some of my associates and want to bring them things too because you are a good lady, but you don't have to any more. Just show up like you normally do."

Jacob had gotten some inside dirt on Michaels and had threatened to expose him if he made Eva continue to bring in the drugs. They were in no shortage of drugs in prison, and what Eva was bringing would not be missed. Michaels just liked the extra money from having something else to sell. However, the dirt Jacob had on him was worth letting her in. The phone line got very quiet.

"Eva…Eva, are you still there?"

"Yes," she said softly.

"What's the matter now?"

"You care."

"I told you that before. Why is that so hard to believe? Is it because of what I've done or is it because of what you've gone through?"

"Both. I know who you are, Jacob. You are a hard man and to love you can be…"

"You don't know who I am. You know what I have become. But you are helping me to figure out who I am, and it's just as scary for me to let you get that close. I don't have room for people. But I will tell you why you turn me on. It is because you are not afraid of me. I don't know anybody that is not afraid of me… Shut the hell up. If that man tells me to get off the phone one more time I will kill him."

"If anybody else had said that I would take it as a figure of speech. I worked too hard to keep you from getting executed, don't hurt anybody while you are there. I will let you go."

"Wait a minute. Are you going to trust me?"

"We are both as shattered as a broken window. We both are going to have to learn to trust somebody. So yes, I'm going to trust you and maybe we can both work through some pain."

"Love you."

"Love you too."

The next morning at ten, Drew and Payton Hill faced off again. "All rise, the court of Honorable Judge Roberts is now in session. You may be seated," said the bailiff.

Payton began, "The prosecution calls to the stand Amanda Henderson, Your Honor."

Drew knew that the only reason that Amanda was being called was to draw sympathy from the jurors. A grieving wife with a long-term hardship could weigh very heavily on the verdict. That is why Payton Hill worked very hard to stir up public sympathy because he knew that some of the same people that had been bombarded by the media would also be the same people on the jury. He also wanted to look good for the public because he was up for re-election.

"Mrs. Henderson, can you please describe your relationship with the deceased?"

"Don Henderson was my husband, my companion, the father of my children and a good friend for eighteen years."

"I know this may be difficult to do, Mrs. Henderson, but can you tell the jury what happened to you on the evening of December 24?

"Don called me and said he would be home later that evening. He had a change in schedule and was asked to do security at Myer Plaza."

"Was this unusual for him?"

"No, he was always taking small jobs. The salary of a police officer sometimes needs support. It was always hard on me not being able to see him, especially on Christmas Eve."

"How did you find out about your husband's death?"

"I was making things for Christmas dinner with the kids, and there was a knock at the door," Amanda started crying, "The officer asked, 'Are you Mrs. Henderson?' I said yes. Then he said, 'I am sorry to inform you that your husband has been killed in the line of duty.' I just screamed after that."

"How will this loss affect your family?"

"We will be financially devastated. Our children may not be able to complete school. It is a terrible loss."

"Did you husband ever mention Mario Reid or Germaine Warren?"

"Yes."

"What did he say about them?"

"Objection, hearsay."

"Sustained."

"What was the relationship between your husband, Reid and Warren?"

"Objection, speculation."

"Sustained."

"How did you know that your husband knew Reid and Warren?"

"Because I had seen them in the patrol car with him on several occasions. He said they were troublemakers, but it would eventually catch up with them."

"Objection, hearsay, Your Honor."

"Sustained, strike the last comment from the records. Mr. Hill…never mind."

"No further questions. The prosecution rests, Your Honor."

Drew began his cross-examination.

"Mrs. Henderson, thank you for taking the stand today," For Drew, this was pure sarcasm. "I am sure this must be very difficult for you. I just have a few questions. Under examination by Mr. Hill you stated that one of your main concerns was the financial implications due to your husband's death. Could you please elaborate on that?"

"Two of our children are in college, and we were struggling already just trying to get them through school. I am in pain for them if we have to discontinue their education. We did have an insurance policy, but that money is needed to pay off the mortgage on the home. I've just been trying to find a way to keep things together," Mrs. Henderson started the tears.

"Mrs. Henderson, do you have any other assets that can be used to fund your children's education if the insurance policy is not enough?"

"Well, I was told that the Officers Memorial Fund often steps in to aide those killed in the line of duty."

Drew knew that he had prepared the bait well, and was about to snap the trap. "Mrs. Henderson, are you familiar with any of these addresses: 1311 Falcon Dr., 2473 Taylor Blvd., and 6719 Contessa Way?" He could feel the tension mounting in the courtroom.

Mrs. Henderson was stunned for a moment. "Uh…yes."

"Can you tell the jury if those homes belong to you and your deceased husband?"

"Yes, those are our homes."

"They aren't investment properties, are they?"

"No."

"These are vacation homes that you and Mr. Henderson owned in different states. Did you know that they are valued at over three hundred thousand dollars each?"

Mrs. Henderson was growing flushed.

"Answer the question, Mrs. Henderson."

"Yes."

The court went in an uproar. Roberts pounded the gavel for order in the court.

"You also own a yacht and a very sizeable bank account, Mrs. Henderson, at several banks. Do you not?"

Henderson did not say anything. "Please answer the question, did those assets belong to you and Mr. Henderson, yes or no."

"Yes."

"This is not the salary of a struggling police officer as you described it, is it?"

The dark side of Mrs. Henderson emerged. She started using four letter words that no person should hear. The judge ordered her silent or face contempt of court charges. Drew looked over at Payton Hill; he was hotter than a firecracker in July. Drew smirked: *should have read your own reports.* "No further questions, Your Honor. I would like to re-examine Dr. Pruitt, Your Honor."

Dr. Pruitt took the stand.

"Dr. Pruitt, do you know what an execution style murder is?"

"Of course."

"Explain it to the jury please."

"It is normally when hands and feet are bound and a fatal wound is issued at close range."

"Dr. Pruitt, look at your photos in exhibit one. Look at the knees and hands of Officer Henderson. Describe the condition of the knees and the wrists."

"They are in a reddened condition, but that could be from anything."

"Anything like kneeling in the snow?"

There was a long pause, Drew repeated his question.

"Dr. Pruitt, anything like kneeling in the snow, wrists bound, and the fatal gunshot wound being delivered in a downward position."

"Yes, that is a possibility."

"Would that be more or less likely than an upward shot fired from someone lying on the front seat of a car and then the bullet went through some factors with no scientific basis turn itself around and enter in a downward position?"

"I would not know what a bullet could do."

"I asked about the likelihood of the event based on your years of observation; is it more or less likely?"

"Less likely."

"No further questions. The defense would like to call its first witness, Your Honor. The defense calls County D.E.A. Detective Eric Larson to the stand."

"Do you know Mrs. Amanda Henderson?"

"Yes."

"Oh my God," Hill uttered.

"Have you ever been sexually involved with Mrs. Henderson?"

He hated Drew for this, but he answered the question very hesitantly.

"Yes."

"How often have you been involved with her?"

"For several years."

"Were you in love with Mrs. Henderson?"

You could feel tension from everyone building up in the room. Larson looked over at her. Amanda was bent on every single word he spoke.

"I had to do it, Amanda."

"You did not answer the question Mr. Larson."

"No. I was not in love with Amanda Henderson."

Mrs. Henderson began sobbing out loud.

"Your Honor, I wish play audio tapes as Defense exhibit two."

"Objection based on content being able to inflame the jury."

"What is the nature of the content, Mr. Jones?"

"These are the interrogation tapes recorded the night Germaine Warren was arrested. The defense wishes to establish that Mr. Warren was under duress at the time of the confession."

Judge Roberts looked at Drew, then he looked at Payton. "The court deems it critical information to the outcome of the case and is not being used to purposely inflame the jurors. Sustained."

"Mr. Larson, have you ever witnessed events like the one I am about to refer to?" Drew began playing the cassettes of the police torturing Germaine. What they heard was grisly—racial slurs and body being beaten and slapped around with phone books. They heard sheer agony. Nothing could have prepared the jurors for this. Drew saw many of them crying, even the media had to go to station break to censor out some of the profane acts.

Mr. Larson answered the question, "Yes."

Drew lined up his missile carefully. "Is this uncommon?"

"No, this is not uncommon."

"Objection! Leading the witness." Hill screamed.

"Overruled."

The newsmen were swarming. Some of the top brass were so humiliated that they began exiting the courtroom. Drew continued; he was about to launch. "Mr. Larson, do you know Antonio Connors?"

"Yes."

"Will you please inform the jury who Antonio Connors is?"

"Connors is a known drug lord that has been under investigation for years."

More buzzing went throughout the courtroom.

"The St. Louis police department did an extensive manhunt in the area where Germaine and Mario lived, is that correct?"

"Yes."

"How would you define *extensive*."

"We pulled all recent arrests records and any other violations of high significance such as felonies and did house-to-house pickups of violators."

"Mr. Connors lived in that area, correct?"

"Yes."

"Was there a reason that Connors was not interrogated?"

"We had only speculative evidence on him."

"How was he more or less speculative than any other felon?"

There was a long pause.

"So the department knew about him, but declined to interrogate him."

"Yes," he said reluctantly.

"Was Officer Henderson under investigation?" You could have heard a pin drop in the courtroom.

"Yes, I was assigned to try to uncover this. I have pretended to be in a relationship with his wife to get closer to the truth." The jury became unglued. The gavel pounded. "We believed that Henderson was involved in large trafficking of cocaine. He was not on assignment that night, and we believe something went wrong."

"How do you know he was not on assignment?"

"I viewed his schedule after the murder because of my hunch."

"Yet, he was in uniform when his body was found."

"Unfortunately, yes."

"Objection!!! Your Honor, where is this going?!"

"Overruled!" Richards ordered.

"Do you believe that Germaine Warren murdered Henderson?!"

"Objection!!! Your Honor, this is clearly speculation and unduly prejucial!"

Judge Roberts took a long hard look at Drew, Larson, and the media. The audience held their breath. "Overruled!" Larson truthfully answered the question, "No, there was no motive and no opportunity."

Drew gave a piercing look to Hill and thought, *"No innocent person should go to jail."*

"Mr. Larson, would the District Attorney's Office have known about Henderson and Connors since you stated that they were under investigation since it would have been their job to press charges?"

"Objection, Your Honor, speculation."

"Overruled."

"Yes."

"No further questions. The defense rests."

"Is the prosecution to cross-examine Mr. Hill?" "No questions, Your Honor."

The St. Louis courthouse had never seen an upset like this one. The entire city was reeling over the idea of corruption, sex, money, drugs and some hotshot black boy named Drew Jones. The news coverage on this case was like no other in the history of St. Louis. Drew was not afraid to bring the depravity of public officials out of the closet. He would never be underestimated in the legal arena after today.

The jury deliberated for thirty minutes and returned a not guilty verdict for Germaine. They also offered an apology. Germaine fell to his knees and thanked God and Drew for this victory. He walked out of that courtroom a free man. Drew was overjoyed. In the midst of all of his happiness, there was still the sting of the enemy because he was well aware of the fact that to save another person's life could mean losing your own.

Chapter 11

The media attention had made Drew a celebrity, and after this exhaustive trial he just felt like getting away from it all. He went to a place too busy to be noticed: the large Galleria Mall. He loved the Galleria because it reminded him of growing up. He often dodged his grandmother's decree to go to church on Sunday by slipping off to the mall. It was the place to be. Everybody in the Boot Heels went there. You could walk around for hours without a dime and nobody would know. If you walked out without anything you would say, "I couldn't find anything that I liked."

Everybody at the mall was on the same playing field because you never knew who had money to spend or who did not. This made for a commission salesman's nightmare, but it was fun. As a matter of fact Drew even contributed his fine dressing to studying mannequins and finding the best high-dollar suits and shoes for less. As he browsed the mall, he prepared to lose the stress of the Henderson case and to relax.

He stopped by one of his favorite gadget stores to even get more lost. As he walked about the store tinkering with various electronic toys, his eyes spotted what he thought would most take him away for the moment. It was a sleek black leather full-body massage chair. He scooted over to it quickly before anyone else could. Turning on the vibrators, he sank himself into the chair, becoming fully emerged in its magical abilities to sooth and comfort. He looked around hoping that the sales people were not keeping track of time. After about five minutes of sheer therapy, he realized that they didn't care so he continued to indulge, this time closing his eyes.

His mind took him slowly away from the frigid St. Louis temperatures and landed him on a beach in Maui; he was just about to sip a Piña Colada when he was interrupted by a delicate voice. "I know you," a woman said. Drew didn't want to open his eyes because since the trial he had heard those words so many times and he thought that just for a moment he had gotten away from everything. But all good things must come to an end, so he slowly opened his eyes and was about to sigh when he saw the sight of someone he thought he would never see again.

"Remember me? I was the lady being assaulted on the stairs that day, and you saved my life. I wanted to die that day and was praying to God that he would just end my life, when he sent you, my angel." Tears began to stream down her face, thank you for speaking out and helping me. I was beaten so badly that I could hardly see you, but I asked God to let me remember you, and he did. I am so grateful that I saw you today."

Drew was speechless; he just reached out and squeezed her hand.

"I saw you at the trial, and I'm glad you did that; at least some of the corruption has been exposed. I hate them, but I know I have to find a place in my heart to forgive them."

Drew pulled out one of his grandmother's favorite sayings, "Time heals all wounds."

She leaned forward and kissed him on the forehead. "Thank you," then she drifted away into the crowded mall. His heart was deeply moved; days like this made it worth it all.

THE DEFENDER

After seeing the lady in the mall, Drew felt he had been as close to heaven as the night he lay beaten in the streets of St. Louis. But instead of seeing an epiphany, he had seen grace and mercy unfolded before his eyes. Not only was the woman alive, but she had a sound enough mind to discuss the horrific encounter without emotionally disintegrating. He realized that it was only the mercy of God that could have brought her through. This left him in a mood to celebrate. So he went to a popular local establishment called The Prep for a Friday night spin on the dance floor; even though he did not consider himself much of a dancer.

Tonight's attendances were members of the Black Bar Association and Black Accountants Association. The Prep felt like a fine New York City stomp. It was the closest thing that St. Louis would ever have that could match the sophistication of the Big Apple. It was so polished that Drew could not even imagine that they would lend themselves to a black audience. Perhaps it was the fact that they were all highly educated and could afford the drinks that they had opened the doors. Someone in the establishment had the insight to know that all blacks were not thugs or dope heads. Everyone in St. Louis knew that if you walked through the doors of The Prep that you were a part of the prestige.

Drew found a seat at the bar and ordered a few drinks. He found himself quite entertained by the impressive group all dressed in black shirts and jeans. Nobody had informed him that you had to be color coordinated. So his jeans were in sync, but his shirt was out of place. Underneath his black leather bomber jacket was a sierra brown shirt. He started to zip the jacket up so that he would match, but it was far too heated from all the dancing bodies to even have such a thought. And it was also getting too hot to look cool by wearing leather.

He was caught between conformity and feeling like a human torch. After much inner debate, he decided to chuck the jacket. He knew he would survive being an oddity. Soon, though, Drew realized that it was only until he became an oddity that he saw action coming his way. She was coffee brown, long haired, perfectly sculptured in jeans, and fine. She was flashing a mesmerizing smile, and Drew had to look around to see if it really was directed towards him. "It must be the shirt," he said, chuckling.

"What's so funny?" she asked.

Drew almost did not know what to say. Her presence was like a great Nubian queen. She was so gorgeous. He wanted this one to be around for a while and carefully thought about what to say.

"To be honest, I was wondering if you were really smiling at me. When I did not see anyone else sitting around me well... I was just laughing at my reaction to your smile."

"No, I was really smiling at the bartender." They both laughed. Then she said. "No really, I saw you sitting over here earlier by yourself, then a little while later you had not moved, so I thought what the heck, no use in both of us being bored."

Drew tilted his head back a little and just looked at her. He was thinking, *She's been noticing me. I am surely out of touch. I have not seen anything but couples on the dance floor dancing like a bunch of aliens.* As badly as he may have wanted the attention of a woman, he was just too consumed with defending to engage in even a small social life.

"I'm DeNita Melrose."

"And I am..."

She interrupted, "Drew Jones."

Lord have mercy, Drew thought to himself, *Celebrity has its perks.*

"The trial was awesome," she continued. "You really do try to stand up for people. When your police brutality pictures showed up on the front page of *The Tribune*, that's when I started following the case. I'm so tied up in my own case load that I…"

"So you're an attorney."

"Yes, I work for Cumberland and Cumberland as their head corporate attorney. You know they just merged with Peacock and Wilson, and I have been swamped with the merger."

Brains and beauty, he thought, *maybe this dance wasn't a total waste.*

Drew offered to buy DeNita a drink, but she remarked that she never drinks while she's out because she has to drive herself home. Drew wished he had abided by that simple policy that night. He was three drinks loaded, but his fascination with the enchanting woman was overriding his lack of sobriety. It was if his brain was saying, *look stupid, I am not going to let you blow this opportunity, under ordinary circumstances I would have your speech slurred by now*. However, he did finish his last drink, because he simply could not bear to waste money even though it would add to being tipsy.

Drew and DeNita talked for hours. They went through everything from where each went to school to why people in St. Louis eat toasted ravioli. He was refreshed to have someone speaking to him outside of legal terms. And not just someone, but a drop-dead gorgeous woman who was already attracted enough to him to engage him in fun conversation. He couldn't tell whether he was more taken by her conversation or her deep dazzling eyes. This was the third taste of heaven that he encountered today. God was good—he had won the case, he had met the angel at the mall, and now he was with DeNita. It was almost too much.

"So what got you involved in law?" asked Drew.

"My fifth grade teacher got our class a subscription to *The Wall Street Journal* and I was fascinated by all of the business transactions that I read about, especially corporate mergers. So when I got older, I learned that there were corporate attorneys and I decided that is what I wanted to do. What about you?"

"My older brother got in trouble with the law for bringing a gun to school."

"What?"

"Yeah, it's a long story, but he was fighting over some girl and brought a gun to school to even up a fight. This happened twice, but the second time my mother could not afford an attorney and she sent me to court with him. After watching the attorney the first case, I just felt compelled to do something so I told the judge I move for him to dismiss the case, and he did."

"You're joking."

"No, I am serious, that was my first case, and I've been hooked ever since."

"That's almost unbelievable, but after watching you operate over the last few weeks, you are bold enough to say or do probably anything. How's your brother now?"

"He's doing all right. He managed to stay out of trouble once he got older. You said you weren't from here, how did you get to St. Louis?"

"I was raised in Silver Springs, Maryland, and went to private school most of my life. My dad is a dentist and drilled us on the importance of a solid education and getting all As in school. When I graduated from law school I was planning on settling there, but some personal issues came up, and I thought it was in my best interest to get a change of atmosphere. Actually it was good move."

"That's pretty impressive. How did your family feel about you moving?"

"They knew it was a good decision and were so excited when I landed my first job. What about your family?"

"I was from a very small town in Sikeston. I grew up around

laborers and sharecroppers, and I knew that was not what I wanted. I made a promise to my mother and my grandmother that I was going to become an attorney and that's what I did."

"They must be very proud of you."

"Well, they would be, but they died right after college a few years a part."

"I'm so sorry to hear that."

"Yeah, it was hard. They meant everything to me, especially my grandmother. She was so inspirational and trusted God for everything. My mother worked so hard to raise us. I wish she could have been there. She knew she was dying of cancer but didn't tell me. I know a lot of things I would have handled differently if I had known.

"Maybe she knew that and did not want you to be different. Sometimes people cope better with impending death when things stay as normal as possible. It keeps them in a normal routine so people won't express feeling sorry for them or treating them more guarded, thus making them focus on what is eminent. She knew you well enough to know what you were going to do and thought it was worth the risk for her peace of mind."

Drew got quiet for a moment. His mind shifted back to a time when he saw his mother extremely happy. She was smiling as she waved good bye, dropping him off on his first day of college. "Psychology might have been fitting as well."

Drew noticed the lights on the dance floor dimming. A throwback from his past, Michael Jackson's "I Wanna Rock with You," was fading away into Luther's "Today and Forever." He reached over and drew DeNita to the dance floor. They locked into a position reserved only for lovers. Drew felt his body tremble at the gentle touch of DeNita as she placed one hand on his shoulder and leaned her head into his chest. Her beautiful scent was more intoxicating than wine. It had been so long since he had been on the dance floor that he found himself intensely focusing on every step. His arms wrapped around her perfectly sized waist. They swayed together like the gentle rocking of the ocean. Luther rolled into Peabo, and Peabo rolled into enough smooth jazz to keep them glued to the floor.

When they finally took time to notice, time had slipped away, and there were only two other couples on the dance floor. They just stood there looking at each other, not quite knowing what to say. Finally, DeNita broke the silence.

"Give me your keys." Drew was too enraptured to respond; she could have asked for anything at that moment. "I'm taking you home." Drew stopped cold.

"No, don't even think it, I'm not that kind of girl, but you've had too much to drink, and the police would just love to pull you over after what you've just done."

"How are you going to get home?"

She flashed that smile again. "You'll just owe me breakfast and a ride in the morning."

Drew's heart almost stopped.

Chapter 12

As they walked to Drew's car, the brisk air brought him to full attention. He was not dreaming. A goddess was about to enter his domain. His mind was racing a hundred miles an hour. How did this happen, especially so quickly? It was an unexpected blessing. When they arrived at Drew's apartment, he apologized for it not being neat. But actually in DeNita's eyes it was neat and cozy. He had good taste.

The front room contained a black leather sofa and chair with red throw pillows. The critical-male-gear entertainment center with assorted audio and visual toys surrounded one wall. Black bar stools flanked the extended counter top that acted as a kitchen table. Another small table and two chairs faced a window that was used as a desk. This room led to an open L-shaped kitchen that had a subdued blue and green wall paper on the walls, with oak cabinets. There were several pictures of his mother and grandmother scattered about and diplomas on the wall. "This is very nice," DeNita remarked.

Drew picked up the remote, zapped on the widescreen TV, and invited DeNita to have a seat. This was the first time in his life that any woman had been in his domain and the relationship was simply platonic. But it was a good feeling. Her saying that she was not that type of girl really caught his attention. He owed her the gesture of kindness the act of being a gentleman. So they chatted until the early hours of the morning.

"Are these pictures of your mother and grandmother?" DeNita asked.

"Yes."

"They had a big influence over you."

"They really did. I ran from some of them. They wanted me to be more spiritual, but at that time I just wasn't ready. But that didn't stop them. See that big black Bible sitting on the table."

"Yeah."

"Well grandma told me to just bring it even if I did not read it. She said she would pray that it got to me even if I never opened it. Well eventually it did. Because every time I would pass by it, it reminded me of how much she wanted me to go to church."

"So are you in church now."

"Yes, I have a good church now and gave my heart to God. What about you? "

"I was born and raised Baptist and spent most of my time singing in the choir. I am in the same church that I was as a child."

"You'll have to sing for me one day."

"No, you'll have to come see me sing but not in church."

"Really?"

"I sing at a karaoke night at Chapman's Restaurant once a month. I sing contemporary Christian songs to influence the young people that are there. I guess you can call it my little ministry."

"That's impressive. What else makes you tick?"

"Being successful—one thing my daddy taught me well was not to hang out with losers. He would say, 'DeNita, you can't hang with turkeys and soar with eagles and in life you are either one or the other.' What did you live by?"

"My folks taught me don't ever be afraid to do the right thing no matter what it cost. It is hard to do some times. But being that way teaches you not to be afraid of people."

"I know you mean that because from what I've seen you are pretty fierce. And it is interesting to see you have a softer side."

"I only bring my claws out when necessary. Those people at work can drive me crazy. So I always have to stay defensive. But you are not a powder puff either, being a lead attorney and doing mergers."

"I like to think of myself as velvet steel."

"That's a good one. I have to remember that so I don't get crushed."

"You, Mr. Jones, would not be the object of my wrath."

"You are quite interesting."

They continued their conversation. Then later watched a classic movie, and fell asleep on the sofa.

Saturday morning, Drew was already up. He picked up a few toiletries for DeNita and drove down to McDonald's to pick up two breakfast platters and some juice. He heard her stirring when he walked in the door. Drew sat down in the chair and just watched in fascination as if he were looking at a Rembrandt. She was as gorgeous asleep as with eyes wide open. Upon the scent of the sausage in the bag, she opened her eyes.

"You cheated."

"What?"

"I said YOU would owe me breakfast and a ride home, not McDonald's."

Drew laughed, "I don't cook."

"You lie." She walked over to the kitchen and pointed to the refrigerator. "May I?"

"Go ahead."

Within it was remnants of the typical bachelor fast-food addiction, but there was some nutrition in there too. She pulled out some eggs, a loaf of bread, and a few pieces of fruit. Then she walked over to him and snatched the breakfast bag out of his hand, pulled out what she wanted, and put the rest in the refrigerator. "Come on," she said smiling. They washed their hands and started cooking. Drew had never made French toast in his life, and it was a lot of fun preparing breakfast with her. They sat down at the table by the window and enjoyed the fresh morning view. Even though they both had a lot of work to do, their fascination with each other made them slip away from it all for the day.

"You are a good cook, Miss Melrose."

"I know it."

"You are just vain."

"No, just successful at everything that I do."

"I believe in positive confessions. That is pretty good. What would you say is the greatest thing you've successfully accomplished since law school?"

"Living here, away from my family. I am very attached to my family, and moving here was a big adjustment for me, but staying here through the years is really challenging. But I've done it successfully, and am really happy to be here."

"I love my family too. My parents divorced while I was young, and then my mom moved us to St. Louis. But DeNita, to be honest I never want to go back home. It is too depressing. I've seen my family struggle so hard. It's like for generations they are stuck. Success to me is allowing them to see that I have made something of myself and hopefully inspire them to come out of drudgery. It is not that they don't have an honest living, but they work so hard and just die. I want to enjoy life."

"Well you are on the right road to do that. I think what you are doing is commendable. You know, my parents shall have been married fifty years next year and I can't wait. Listening to you makes me realize how fortunate I am."

"Whenever I do get married, I don't want to go through what they did. It is too hard, especially on children."

"Good for you, Mr. Jones, good for you."

"You've been a bright spot in my day today. Thanks for bringing me home."

He drove DeNita back to her car just before sunset. "You drive a Spider?"

"No I lease a Spider. When I get finished paying for law school then I will buy a Spider."

What have I gotten myself into—a classy woman down to her car? I am embarrassed to have a princess riding around in a Honda."

"At least your Honda is paid for."

They both laughed and exchanged phone numbers before she left. Drew ended their brilliant day with a kiss on the hand. This had to be different.

Chapter 13

Things at the Public Defender's Office seemed to go on as usual over the next months after the fanfare of the Henderson case had died down. A few of the attorney's were feeling pressure due to some of Richardson's case load being shifted. Drew was feeling a pinch of that but he was so caught up in his fascination with DeNita that it seemed to make things a lot more bearable. Eva Richardson's emotional state seemed to deteriorate daily. Blake tried to help Eva as much as he could, but things were not getting better for her. It all came to a head when Blake got an anonymous phone call concerning Eva. It took him a few days to investigate the matter, but the conclusion was not what he wanted. He called Eva into his office and what happened left them both in tears.

"Eva, how on earth did you get involved with…of all people Jacob Black? Do you know what this means I am going to have to do?"

Eva was crying so hard she could barely speak.

"I know, Blake, and I know that you were trying to help me. I'm just so sorry. I am so sorry, Blake."

"Eva, what happened?"

"Katherine had the baby, and it was a little girl," she said weeping.

"Who is Katherine?"

"David had an affair with one of his students."

"Oh my God."

"It went on for three years, Blake. I was so humiliated but always thought it will be over soon. But it wasn't. So one day I finally got tired and went to confront him…"

"And you saw her…" Blake got out of his chair and walked around his office with his hand over his mouth.

"I wanted to get back at him so bad. I just wanted to hurt him as badly as he hurt me…"

Blake walked over to Eva and placed his hand on her shoulder. "I'm so sorry this happened to you. Why didn't you ask for help?"

"Do you know how hard it is having my reputation of always being on top of things and at the top of my game then to have people know that I really have issues and that my husband cheated on his perfect little wife? I was too embarrassed and devastated to share this with anyone, especially Katherine being pregnant and some people here already knew I wanted a child."

"I am devastated too, Eva, you knew that you meant the world to me. I have been so fortunate to have you as one of my best attorneys."

"Just knowing that I have disappointed you, Blake, makes me feel awful. But I had no idea I was going to wind up so emotionally involved with Jacob. I couldn't even stop it. I just kept going back to him."

"You might want to consider some counseling."

"You are probably right. I lived for eight years in a terrible marriage, and the thought that it took Jacob to make me feel needed and loved ought to let you know how bad it was for me."

"Oh my God."

"But I will tell you this, Blake, I know he is a ruthless and dangerous man, but after getting to know him I found out a lot about what contributed to him being that way and I really think that is why we connected so deeply because we have both been hurt so terribly bad."

Blake just shook his head.

"Eva, I've already called a few people and sent them your résumé. Two colleges that I know need an adjunct teacher for their law school, and I can't think of a better person for the job. Getting away from all of this might do you some good. One of the colleges is in New York and the other is in Boston. Here are their cards, and I hope you will at least look into it."

"Thank you, Blake. I think I will just take a few weeks off and give them a call."

"Okay, I will let them know that."

"Do you mind if I just leave today, Blake?"

"You can leave now if you want to. I will get Calvin and Drew to pack up your things, and you can come in over the weekend when people are not here to get anything they may have left behind. I am going to pay you for vacation and you have three weeks of it."

"I will always appreciate you."

"Just keep in touch, okay."

Eva nodded, grabbed a few tissues to wipe her eyes and then left. Blake called his secretary and told her to cancel any appointments he had for the rest of the day and said that he would be leaving early. He sat at his desk just numb. About an hour later he called Calvin and Drew into his office. They immediately saw how shaken he was.

"I might take a day off tomorrow. I will have to see how I am feeling later on this evening, but for now I am going home," Blake said.

"Are you feeling ill? Calvin asked.

"I just terminated Eva."

"Blake, I am sorry," said Drew. Calvin was too stunned to speak. He knew Eva was doing poorly but not to the point of termination without at least being written up or put on probation. "I thought we were helping her to get caught up?"

"I had to let her go. She got involved with Jacob Black."

The room got eerily silent for a few moments.

"Bad Blood?" Calvin asked.

"Yes."

"Her husband got a student pregnant that he was having a long term affair with and she got involved with Jacob to get back at him and unfortunately it backfired and she got emotionally bonded to Jacob."

"That is terrible and explains why her files started falling a part almost a year ago. Did the girl have the baby?" said Calvin.

"Yes."

"How could she get emotionally tied to a man that would dip his food in his victim's blood and eat it?" Drew said shockingly.

One of the most notorious clients in prison was Jacob Black. He had been renamed by the inmates as Bad Blood for doing the sickest thing imaginable. He allegedly knifed an eighty-year-old woman forty-seven times and was so calloused to the murder that he went out and took some of the money that he robbed her for to buy a box of chicken. Then he returned, sat down, and ate the chicken in the presence of the corpse, dipping the chicken in her blood like it was barbeque sauce. As revolting as this person was, Richardson loved him.

"Drew, there is no fury like a woman scorned. She wanted to hurt him bad, and that at the time it was the vilest thing she could think of," Blake said. "I don't want this around the office. Please keep this to yourselves. I got an anonymous tip and I don't know who else knows, but I just don't want you to spread anything."

"You know we wouldn't do that, Blake," Calvin said.

"I know, but I just want you to hear me say it. I want you all to stay after work today and clean out her office. Please wait until everybody leaves before getting started."

"She's already gone?" said Drew.

"She asked is she could leave today and I told her now, if she wanted to."

"What is she going to do?"

"I'm recommending her to a few law schools, and I told her she just might need to get away for a while."

"Poor thing," said Calvin, "This is tragic."

"I hate this," Drew said.

"So if I am not here tomorrow, you will know why. I just need some time to process this. I don't know if anyone really realizes how much time I've invested in her. She's been with us ten years and is like a daughter to me. This is all a bit much."

"We will take care of things," Calvin said, and with that he and Drew left the office.

Everybody felt the overload from Richardson's cases. You could tell the very point when she became involved with evil because her cases went from being detailed and orderly to complete incoherence. The one Drew hated the most was her leaving a man in jail for quite some time without even visiting him. He could just imagine how out of control she was and little by little just left things completely undone.

This man had been accused of robbing a Payless Shoe Store. He was locked up, and not a single attorney had visited him. There were no witnesses to the robbery; there were no surveillance tapes because, according the store manager, it was not working that day. As a matter of fact the only person who saw the criminal was the store manager. The following day after the robbery, the manager quit the job. But, just before leaving when the police had beat the streets down for any suspect, he said, "Yeah, that's him."

This was the end of the case. Nothing else was done. Just an unfounded accusation and a man left in jail for almost a year with no intervention as a result. The prosecutor had even admitted that he felt the manager was the robber. Yet, they had no compassion on a man's ruined life. Drew was furious. He went to the prosecuting attorney and said if that man was not released at the end of the day, he would have every news media in St. Louis on the case. The man was released by the prosecutor, and all charges were dropped. Their office did not need any more media attention at this time.

Drew went home that evening more exhausted than ever. Richardson's additional cases had taken their toll on him, and the Payless matter was just another unwanted reminder of unnecessary corruption. For the first time in his life, he began to wonder if his dream of defending lives was really worth it because the injustice in the system was in his eyes worse than the alleged criminals he was charged with defending. They were the ones who really needed to be in jail. He flopped on the sofa and felt at least this day would be different because he could pick up the phone and have a pleasant encounter awaiting him on the other end. DeNita had been hoping that he would call.

"You sound awful," she said.

"Yeah, this has been a pretty rough day. Have you ever wondered if you made the right career choice?"

"Yeah," DeNita answered, "All the time. People think that the life of a lawyer is full of money, luxury, and easy living, but it's not. In my field of corporate law I see people doing things every single day that are at the edge of illegal. It bothers me, but technically they are not committing a crime. They just don't see any problems with stretching the legal rope to the snapping point."

"Did you anticipate that going in?"

"Not to the extent that I have experienced it, what about you?"

"To be honest, DeNita, I feel like resigning. Then I shake myself and say but if all the good people leave what happens to those people who are really innocent and just don't have the means to help themselves? I know that I am not their only hope, but I also know that I am a hope for them. Just like today, I got a man out of jail that had been sitting there almost a year without ever having seen an attorney."

"How did that happen?"

"The attorney assigned the case just never got around to doing anything for the man because she was in a state of depression after being jilted by her husband. To make matters worse she found out that the mistress was pregnant. Oh, DeNita, this is twisted. She was so angry for what he did that she got involved sexually with one of the vilest persons in the county jail and fell in love with him. She was not planning on that, she was just trying to hurt her husband. The sad thing was, she was an excellent attorney and will be sorely missed. "

"That's incredible! Did Blake take it pretty hard?"

"He was so devastated he went home and said he may not come in tomorrow. He really loved her."

"All this extra work is draining the hell out of me. I feel so bad for her," Drew said.

"You know what I do after I've had a day like yours? Something very simple, I just take a walk, a nice long walk. It's amazing what a little fresh air will do to clear your mind. It does not make the problems go away but it sure helps you to handle them better."

"Anything would be worth helping me to get out of this funk."

"I'd love to join you," DeNita said, "But I have a function that I have to attend if I want to keep my career. But I usually go to Avondale Park. When you get there, why don't you call me on your cell phone, and we will finish this conversation while I am getting ready to go."

"A phone date—never had one of those," Drew laughed. "Okay, I'll call you back in a little bit."

Blake went home that afternoon wishing that Arlene was there. He knew she had late hearings and would probably not get home until after dinner hour. Eva's situation got him thinking about a lot of things. It started with thoughts of Arlene. She and Blake had known each other for years. When they first met, Blake wanted to date her, but she knew that he had a reputation of being a ladies man and did not want to become part of his collection. So they remained casual friends. But she had always captivated him and he told himself that if he ever decided to settle down and she was available he would pursue her.

When he turned fifty, he had an inward change of nature. He knew he did not want to stay on that same road. It took almost two years to fully pursued Arlene that he was serious.

Seven months ago, he proposed and she moved into his condo. He began to reminisce on they day they got engaged. They were in the middle of the Gulf of Mexico on a Royal Caribbean Cruise for a much needed week of vacation.

The balmy breeze and starry black velvet sky set a perfect mood as the two of them stood on the balcony of their suite. Blake reached in his pocket and pulled out a multi-tear diamond band.

"Told you I always get what I want," he said reaching over and sliding the band on to her finger. *"So presumptuous that you don't need to pop the question?"* Blake smiled, *"You know a good thing when you see it. I'm only doing this once."*

"Hate to bust your little bubble but um, you didn't get what you wanted. I hooked you the day I told you no I was not willing to become a part of your harem. I knew you were the type of man that could not handle no. All I had to do was to wait."

"Looks like to me that we both got what we wanted. I just wish I had done this sooner," Arlene wrapped her arms around Blake and kissed him. "I love the ring and you have made me a very happy woman for the last two years."

Then his mind slipped back to the conversation with Eva. He wondered about many things. Eva's situation brought blaring realities to his face. He never realized the devastation affairs can cause until he saw how Eva had deteriorated. A woman's career was needlessly ended over matters of the heart. Now his heart was bleeding. His mind weaved through different transitions for hours. When he heard Arlene finally come through the door, he was so relieved.

"Why are you sitting here in the dark?" Arlene said, flipping on the switch in the well-furnished living room.

"I came home early."

She walked over and sat next to him with a puzzled look, "Are you okay?"

"Let me ask you something. If I wanted us to get married tomorrow would you do it?"

"Blake what's the matter?"

"I had to terminate Eva Richardson today, because I found out and confirmed that she was sleeping with an inmate."

"Oh no, is that the lady that you told me was always a work horse and pretty much stayed to herself."

"Yes."

"How did that happened and what does that have to do with us getting married? I thought we had settled that we were getting married in November."

"She got involved with the guy because her husband was cheating and got his girlfriend pregnant. She wanted to get back at him and thought sleeping with a contemptible person would hurt him as bad as she had been hurt."

"Oh my Lord."

"But when I looked at her I said to myself, how many husbands have I destroyed when they found out their wife was involved with me? How many hearts have I broken? I had never come face to face with the other side of my virility. It shook me up, Arlene, it really did. You know I cared about Eva. I have groomed her for ten years."

"I am so sorry to hear this, and wish it was something I could do. You can't go around regretting your past. You can't change it, Blake."

"I can't change my past, but I can make things right, now. You know I've lived with other women before, and there is really no difference in what we are doing and what I've done. Because either of us could walk out at any minute because the only solid connection in my mind is marriage. I've never been engaged before, but as of today that is still not enough. My problem has been not being willing to commit to anyone long term. I have you and that's what I want. I want to know that I am completely settled and November is too long."

"You are serious."

"I have never been more serious in my life. We can still have a formal ceremony in November but I want you now. When I saw how much pain Eva was in, just to get some man to love her and how it drove her to an extreme state of mind to sacrifice everything for love. That was too much for me. I know you are going to marry me. But I need to commit now, totally. We can fly to Las Vegas tonight and get married tomorrow."

Arlene had never seen Blake this way. He was always a very composed and in control man. She just held him and said okay. Then they both called their office and left messages that they had a family emergency and took the last flight to Vegas on Southwest Airlines.

They got married in a small one-room white cottage that was converted into a chapel. The cottage was in the middle of a flower garden. The inside of the chapel had a solid glass wall behind the altar looking out at the flower garden. It was a beautiful sight. The inside was decorated in white silk covers laid over church pews, and the room was filled with chandeliers. There was a white marble floor, and the walls were painted red. They two of them were dressed very simply. He wore a dark blue suit with a burgundy tie. She had on a pretty form-fitting white dress that reached her ankles. She wore her hair pinned up with soft red curls flowing around her face. She was carrying a bouquet of wine-colored roses.

"I now pronounce you husband and wife. You may now kiss your bride."

Blake leaned over and kissed Arlene as if this was the last day of his life. He would not stop kissing her. Finally the preacher had to interrupt. They all laughed. Then he picked her up and carried her out of the chapel. They had a few people on staff taking digital pictures. They waited until they printed the pictures of the ceremony and them walking out of the chapel and then left.

They decided to spend one more night in Vegas and try to be back to work by one the next day. They got in their rental car and went back to their hotel.

Blake said to Arlene, "I just want you for the rest of the time we are here. I don't want to go anywhere else and I don't want to do anything. I just want you."

She spent the rest of her time giving him the security that he needed. Nothing mattered to her more. "You have made me the happiest woman alive."

A few weeks passed, and Drew's encounters with DeNita were becoming more and more frequent and helpful. She had impressed him tremendously, and he felt that she would be someone that his mother and grandmother would have approved of. He even found that he was beginning to like having a bad day, so that it would be an excuse to go walking with DeNita. It was wonderful getting to know someone that Drew felt had his heart.

He sat at his desk privately allowing his mind to be carried away by the first time he had kissed her while sitting on a park bench. Everything in his mind was going in slow motion. He felt every single exhilarating move and could smell her seductive perfume. That kiss seemed to linger forever, but was suddenly interrupted by Blake Adams passing by.

"Drew, you've been doing a great job. I am sorry that Richardson's work load almost ran all of us into the ground, but I just wanted you to know that we hired another attorney to take her place."

Drew nodded in response.

"She was one of my prized attorneys," Blake said lowering his head.

"I know, but no one would have expected that kind of behavior from her."

"You guys are like my family, Drew, and a part of me grows when you grow and a part of me dies when you die." Drew really wanted to say something that would help Blake to heal, but he knew this was a time when no words would matter, so he just stood up, patted him on the back, and said, "We all really appreciate you, Blake, and I personally look up to you and always will."

A gentle smile rolled across Blake's face, and he walked on.

"Thanks, Drew. I really mean that." Drew felt that he, at least, brought a bit of happiness to Blake that day. Seeing Blake smile and knowing that it was Friday was all Drew needed to have a good weekend. He headed for the courthouse to finish up a few sentencing and probation revocation hearings, and then he would head home for the weekend.

Upon his return back from the courthouse to pick up a few files before heading home, he saw a crowd around the door of the defender's office. As he drew closer, he could hear people crying. *Good Lord*, he thought to himself, *What now?* He saw Calvin Row and pushed though the crowd to get to him so he could find out what was going on. As he got closer to Calvin, he saw tears streaming down his face and his hand was over his mouth.

"What happened?" he asked, seeing the backs of a few diligently working paramedics to lift a body onto a stretcher.

"Blake is dead."

Drew was stunned; he pushed through the crowd a little more and was able to get a glimpse of Adams' face before they covered it. "He had a heart attack," Row cried. Drew was too shaken to have a response; he had just spoken with Blake less than two hours ago.

His mind faded back to the day Blake had called him and offered him the job, then it flashed to all the times he had supported him through his worst trials and finally he saw the smile. This moment was so overwhelming for everyone. They all cared about Blake and were now all grieving together. A good man was dead. Drew thought, *Is this how it ends? You work your ass off trying to be a decent man in a corrupt legal system helping persons that no one else would bother too and then you die. Was this the Promised Land that he had set out for?* Speechless, Drew stayed until they took Blake's body away.

Chapter 14

All of the regalia of Blake's funeral could not overshadow that it was a sad day for everybody. The police escort service was designed for a king; dignitaries from all over St. Louis said their words of special condolences, and Calvin Row even got up and said words that moved the crowd to laughter. But it was still a very sad day. Blake would be missed. People often say that anyone is replaceable, but Drew knew that no one would have said that about Blake Adams. You might find a replacement for his position, but you would never find a replacement for the man of value that he was.

This whole event had spiraled Drew back to a place of self inspection. Is what he was sacrificing his life for worth it? Would he too just fall over and die? It was too much for him to handle. After the funeral, Calvin Row walked over to Drew and gave him a hug.

"You know Blake really liked you. I was kind of warming up to you myself, but now since Blake is dead, I don't know what to think of you." He always found a way to lighten things up. In Drew's eyes, Calvin was a saint who didn't have to die to become one.

"How is Arlene taking all of this? To loose your fiancé must be absolutely devastating. It's like going from the highest high to the lowest low," Drew said.

Calvin leaned over and whispered something in Drew's ear.

"What? That is awesome."

"That's one good thing that Eva Richardson did for him. He was so shook up he realized time was too precious to waste."

Calvin told Drew that the day of Blake's conversation with Richardson that he and Arlene flew to Las Vegas and had a private ceremony that they had intended to keep secret and have a formal wedding in November. He also had bought a one-million-dollar life insurance policy for Arlene as a wedding gift to signify that not only will I take care of her for the rest of his life, but thereafter also.

"You know we need you back," Calvin said and then drifted away into the crowd. Drew had not noticed that people saw the change in his disposition after Blake's death. Knowing that someone else cared helped him. Just as Calvin was about to get into his car, he heard a woman crying in the distance. He looked around and saw a woman with a big black hat on and a black two-piece suit standing on the other side of the cemetery facing Blake's grave. He turned around.

"Eva?"

She didn't say anything, she just nodded. Calvin ran to her. She collapsed in his arms and cried. He just held her.

"I miss him so much. I am having a hard time dealing with this. I knew he was under a lot of stress and what I did didn't help at all."

"Nothing anybody could have done would have changed all of this. It was just his time. You know that. You didn't have to be here alone today. We all love you. We just want you to get better."

"Thank you, Calvin," she said, still crying, "I appreciate that."

"What are you going to do from now?"

"Blake helped me to get the job at a university in Albany, New York. I start next month."

"What about Jacob?"

"We decided to stay in contact. I know that is hard for people to understand. But he was there when I wanted to kill myself when I found out about David's baby. He's still there now. And in my mind, with him being in prison for life is good for me, because I know he will always be there—a part of me needs something stable. I don't fully understand my emotions, but that's just the way it is."

"I can respect that, Eva, and I wish you the best. If you ever need anything and I mean it, just call. I told Drew one time that we might care about people that work with us, but we never get involved when we see them hurting because that just the way things work. But after seeing what you've gone through that is a mistake and I want to be there for you now."

Eva hugged Calvin. Gave him a kiss on the cheek and then walked away.

As Drew turned to head towards his car, he saw DeNita standing there. She was the ray of sunlight for him on this dreary day.

"You knew Blake?" Drew asked as he reached her.

"No, but I knew you would be here, so I left work early hoping to catch you. I know this has been a bit much for you and thought that you needed a distraction."

Drew felt his body melting as she wrapped her arms around him, lifted her face, and kissed him. He had been quite the gentleman with DeNita, but that kiss made him desire to be a man with his woman. He was having a difficult time figuring out what language she was speaking. Was it sympathy? Then she whispered, "I want you…"

That evening DeNita became a total distraction to Drew. He

had invited her over to his apartment for dinner and a dip in the indoor pool. It felt so good to hold this work of art in his arms and just float. If anyone else was in the pool that night, neither Drew nor DeNita noticed. Their world became very small. Their focus became each other. And their lips kept defining the focus. Each kiss deeper until Drew felt it was all he could take. Pulling DeNita out of the water, he led her to his apartment.

They eagerly anticipated the unlocking of the door. As it slammed shut behind them, they found themselves frantically peeling off the few articles of clothing that covered them.

"You are beautiful," Drew whispered drawing DeNita into his embrace. They kissed. He carefully backed up to the sofa and pulled her on top of him. It had been so long since Drew had been with a woman that he was about to explode even before she positioned herself and slowly rode him into euphoria. Their actions became so intense, deep, harmonious in rhythm. When she no longer had energy to be upright, she laid herself on his chest. Their kisses were heated. Drew wrapped his arms around her back for one last roll. She moaned, slightly lifting her head, each releasing passionate sounds of ecstasy, collapsing—both were exhausted, but wanted more where nothing was left to give.

Drew felt things he was always previously afraid to speak of. But this moment left him totally vulnerable.

"DeNita, I love you."

"I know," she whispered. "I love you, too."

He held her through the night and prayed that the sun not come up because his dream would end.

The next few weeks after Blake Adams's untimely death was sheer madness for everyone in the Public Defender's Office. There was so much chaos that no one fully got the chance to grieve. Everything that Blake had worked so hard to accomplish with his team hinged on the next person assigned to leadership.

As far as Drew and the other attorneys were concerned the only person worthy for the position was Calvin Row. He had been Blake's shadow and was instrumental in helping him to keep the ship running smooth and efficiently. So when the news came down the pike that Calvin was only going to be assigned as the interim director a wave of frustration and near-mutiny pulsed throughout the department. He was too black to be in the "good old boys" club.

The system had just launched a missile that was bound to wreck this ship. Their oversight of the genius of Calvin Row, the almost never-ending fallout from Eva Richardson's betrayal, and the death of Blake Adams was too much for the overworked, depressed staff. Once a defense attorney loses his reasons to fight for the common good, for the Constitution, then it becomes a game of survival. The worst lawyer to have is one who is just surviving. That lawyer is death to anyone in need of public defense. The poor in need of defense do not stand a chance if their public representative is feeling screwed. They get the worst or the indifferent. After a few weeks, it was apparent that the St. Louis court system did not care.

Drew was livid when he found out that Calvin did not get the promotion. Calvin was taking the low road, but Drew was beginning to get under Calvin's skin just a little to stir him up.

"Did you even ask why they are the bringing in the hick from the Ozarks, when you've been Blake's shadow for years? If you weren't doing an excellent job they would have brought the good old boy in a long time ago, don't you think? You are competent, educated, well trained and respected. What else do they want? Give me one reason, with your credentials, that this is anything more than a racial move."

"Drew, I know this place is political, but it's only a few us here and I don't want to become marked as making trouble. I know how to be an excellent attorney, but I value my own personal peace of mind rather than a fight. I'm not like you, Drew, you don't mind a fight."

"That's probably why they did it then, because they knew you would not say anything. 'Cause I will be damned if it's over your credentials."

"What did you say?"

"I said they know that you are not going to say anything."

"Drew they already made the decision."

"I know, but at least they will know that you were insulted and despise their racist actions. And if they ever overlook you again you will at least file a claim with EEOC to get under their skin, even if it doesn't do any good. Neither one of us would even be standing in this office if someone had not stood up and fought for our rights. You told me once that you pick your battles wisely. If this is not a cause for battle, what is?"

Drew stirred Calvin enough to get him at least to ask questions. First, he was told that he did not have enough experience. So he found out how long the new individual had worked and it was seven years less experience than he had. Then they told him that he had the same position that Blake had in his former location and that it was a lateral move. Calvin investigated that and found it was not so. Finally he was told that due to the ongoing stress in the office and his closeness to the loss of Blake that he would not have the ability to quickly adjust to the new demands and that this individual is far enough removed to do so.

Calvin thought, *That is the most ridiculous thing I have heard yet.* So he wrote his superiors this letter:

It concerns me greatly that I was not considered for permanent replacement of Blake Adams based on your statement as to why the position was not offered. I would rather have been measured by my workmanship, merit, performance and ability rather than your perception that I would not be able to quickly adjust to new demands based on the recent loss of Mr. Adams. However, I was selected to quickly adjust as interim manager and have thus far succeeded in that capacity based on my last performance review. I will be turning all correspondence between your department and my inquiries to other authorities for review of this case. I will also document any negative shifting in my performance ratings after this memo due to my fourteen years of outstanding performance records.

Calvin felt relieved after he had written the letter. He reflected on the time when he had more fight in him. But years of constant battles seemed to drain it away little by little. He had found solace in his comfort zone. He picked up his phone and called Drew.

"I sent the letter."

"Good. There've had enough people to walk out already. They are not going to want you to leave."

"Drew, at this point, even if they did I would be all right. When they told me I couldn't adjust, yet they pitched me in as interim; that was enough. Thanks for getting me out of my comfort zone."

"No problem man."

Within months of Jason Arlington's arrival, the best and most dedicated public defenders abandoned ship. The Public Defender's clients got shafted. Many innocent people would face years in prison or death because of this ill-fated, prejudiced move.

When the new director came aboard, he brought a host of his buddies to replace the attorneys that had left. These young southern lawyers were out of place in an urban culture. They did not understand life in St. Louis and that soon proved to be a mistake…

The Public Defender's Office was always full of players. Every person had a role in the way things operated. There were those who were paid to be there to perform a job and there were others that just loved to hang around the office for whatever reason. Damon Waters was one of those characters. Everybody from the old school knew he was a hell-raiser. He was a former Vietnam veteran on disability. The war had messed him up. Several days a week he would just show up at the Public Defender's Office just to have any type of controversial conversation he could think of for the day. There were certain lawyers that he just loved to spark. This week he was enraged over the mistreating of a young eighteen-year-old black boy that the police had picked up.

When Damon got on his bandwagon, he could get pretty belligerent. But he wasn't a troublemaker. He'd been coming around the office for three years before Arlington arrived. Jason Arlington had seen him several times that day and tried shooing him off. That really seemed to get under his skin.

"That's what I'm talking about," Damon raged. "The white man is always messing with you. That's why I can't stand his ass."

Drew left his desk and went over to Damon, trying to calm him down.

"Man, I know you feel that way. We've got lots of problems in this world. You can stay in here with me until you calm down. I know you've got a lot to say."

"That's all right, Jones, I'm staying right here. He's not going to tell me what to do. This is a public place. I've got a right to be here."

Arlington walked over to one of the sheriffs. "You're going to stand there and not do anything? He is wasting my attorney's time. Get him out of here!"

The sheriff hesitated. "He's not going to bother anybody...let's just give him a few minutes."

"I said, get him out of here!"

THE DEFENDER

The sheriff calmly walked over to Damon, "You've got to leave the building."

"I ain't going anywhere. He don't know me. That's why that boy got locked up; somebody trying to tell him what to do, and he wasn't doing anything. This is a free country. I can talk to anybody I want to. I paid for this country to be free. Better leave me alone."

Arlington just kept screaming, "Get him the hell out of here! And get a restraining order on this idiot."

"I ain't no idiot—I'm a man!" A couple of other sheriffs came over and dragged Damon out of the office and threw him on the streets.

The attorneys who knew him just sat around shaking their heads. Drew watched as the doors closed behind him. He could see out the window that Waters was standing on the street with his fist balled. He knew it did not have to go down that way. Arlington was not informed nor did he care to be. He was in charge now, and things would be done his way. In his economy, there was no room for public interaction; this was a workplace. No diversion, just a workplace. You could see the smug arrogance on Arlington's face as he watched Damon being dragged from the building and tossed out the door. People would now understand that he was in charge. "Get back to work," he ordered. Drew felt like walking out.

When Drew returned to work the next day he found things quite different. All of the non-employees who added color and variety to their days were gone. After what they all saw happened to Waters, they just choose not to return. The Public Defender's Office was now a bona fide workplace. It was so quiet. Arlington never said much to anybody. But today he announced that "we all needed to discourage 'interference' from the 'outside population.'"

Drew went to the dictionary shortly after Arlington's speech to see who he felt was the real idiot by definition. *Let's see,* he thought, *okay it says a born fool, that doesn't fit Waters, utterly senseless or stupid, that doesn't fit Waters, but it does resemble Arlington. Well at least in my opinion.* He smiled.

Within a few months, he had caused the depletion of critical attorneys, which increased workload; removed the points of interest that he considered idiotic; and brought in people who had never experienced the depravity of certain urban living. Now, he had commanded everyone just to come to work and avoid outside influences which were what kept some much needed humor in their domain.

Drew mentally shut down for the day. He was seething over what had happened to Waters. This man had served his country, was now a reject to society, and just wanted was a little conversation to feel as if he mattered. Everyone seemed to have realized this except for the young hick. This was supposed to be a day for Drew to catch up on some paperwork since he did not have a trial. But all he could think about was seeing Waters tossed on the street. Finally, he picked up the phone and invited DeNita over for lunch.

"If you are calling me in the middle of the day it must be a problem," DeNita observed.

"No, I just wanted to invite you over to have lunch with me today."

"Drew you are a workaholic, you don't invite me to lunch. You invite me to dinner after work."

"Okay, you're right. There are just a few things going on here. I need to get out of the office for a bit, and your little magic will keep me sane for the rest of the day."

"Is this about that Waters guy you were telling me about last night?"

"Some of it is. I just can't stand to see people humiliated just because they are poor and don't fit the makeup of normal society. I feel like quitting sometimes."

"There are a lot of people that need you Drew; you can't do that. I need you."

Drew became silent for a moment, those words felt so good to him. "Thank you, DeNita. I needed that."

"Besides you can't quit, anyway."

"And why is that?"

"You remember what you told me about the day you got hired."

"I forgot about that."

"That was the best lines I ever heard: What would it take for you to leave the defender's office, Mr. Jones?"

Drew laughed, "Okay, I said I would leave if someone came in and shot the place up with a machine gun—but he would have to do it twice."

"Love you," DeNita said, "I'll see you in a little while."

He hung up the phone with his burden lifted.

Somehow Drew was able to get himself focused enough to work on a few files. The amount of people in need of Public Defense seemed endless. Before he knew it, it was almost lunch time and he was looking forward to spending time with DeNita. Their schedules kept them so busy that any time he could squeeze in with her was precious.

He fought his mind daily just trying to keep their intimate moment from surfacing at work. She said she wanted to be a distraction for him, but she could never image how much of a distraction she had become. He could be in the middle of a trial and visualize every inch of her undressed wet body. When he was alone, it was almost an obsession. She had unlocked his heart, and it felt good. Since it was almost lunch he allowed himself to be caught up just a little in one of their embraces…until he heard the firing of an automatic and screams of terror.

"Get down! Get down!" he could hear someone yelling amidst the rounds of bullets hailing. *Pop! Pop! Pop!* More screams. *Oh my God, DeNita.* Drew ran towards the door but could not pass because bullets were flying everywhere. He heard someone screaming, "I'm a man. I'm not some damn idiot! I'm a man!" He saw blood spreading across the floor coming from Arlington's office. Two sheriffs were slain. A few attorneys that had stepped out of their offices to escape were being hit by the fire. "Oh my God!" Drew said to himself. Just then he saw Waters running down the hall towards the elevator.

Before he could push the button, the door opened and Drew saw DeNita standing there. Waters grabbed her and put a gun up to her head. She shrieked with terror. She was shaking uncontrollably.

"Don't anybody come near me or I will kill her!" Drew's heart stopped. He had to do something, yet at the same time he was praying that no one else would do something stupid. You could hear people sobbing, and blood was everywhere.

Drew crawled out the door and called out to Damon.

"Mr. Waters! That one is mine please let her go!" He was hoping that the man that answered would not be the demon that was controlling Waters.

Their eyes locked.

For just a moment, Drew knew that he saw Waters and not a demon. He was hoping that the kindness he had always showed towards this man would briefly be remembered, and it was. Waters pushed DeNita to the ground, turned the gun to his own head, and pulled the trigger. Blood splattered all over DeNita as his limp body fell besides her, crossing the elevator door. She had balled herself into fetal position and became hysterical.

THE DEFENDER

At that moment, everything went into overdrive for Drew. The next thing he remembered was picking DeNita up and carrying her to his car. He didn't even remember the drive home or opening the apartment door. They were both catatonic. All he remembered was hearing the shower. When he walked down the hall, DeNita was standing in the shower with all her clothes on scrubbing the blood out of her hair and crying. The blood stains on her clothes were already washed away by the pouring water. Drew stepped in, put his arms around her, kissed her, and cried.

"I cannot lose you."

Chapter 15

The phone never stopped ringing. Everybody wanted to know if he and DeNita were okay. Finally Drew just unplugged the phone. They were still in shock in the bed watching the horror of the day unfold on the evening news. Arlington was dead. Two sheriffs were dead. One was Alexander DuPont, whom Drew had seen raping the inmate in the corridor. The other two had gotten flesh wounds. Seven attorneys were dead, several others were injured.

"When I saw that gun to your head today..." Drew said leaning over on DeNita. "I knew if something had happened to you that would have been the end of me. My emotions have not been ripped like that since my grandmother died. Then I was angry because I said all this could have been avoided if they had given Calvin a promotion and left Waters alone. Nobody that knew him considered him trouble. You can't wound a man's dignity."

"Drew, baby, no, don't feel that way. What if one of the victim's wives heard you say that? They would say, he should have never been allowed in the building and blamed all of you for allowing him to stay."

"Our nation dropped the atom bomb to end the war, DeNita, but that never would have happened if there had not been Pearl

Harbor. There is initial cause and effect."

"It solves nothing, Drew, to wonder why things happen. You can keep going back to find the root, but you never will get to the bottom. Waters would not have been unstable at all if he had not gone to war. How far can this go back, Drew? Let your anger go. It is not worth it. Calvin would be angry if he heard you say that. We are blessed to be alive. They say that your life flashes before your eyes when you face death and that you remember what you regret not doing. I didn't see my life. I saw yours and how much you risked that for me. You mean everything to me and if the last person's face that I saw would have been yours..."

He silenced her with a kiss. "I don't want to ever have to think about not seeing you."

"This is the first time that I realized in my life that tomorrow is not promised and that all you really have is this moment because in an instant life can change. Hand me my purse over there; I want you to hear something."

DeNita reached in her bag and pulled out her iPod and mini speakers.

"Drew, I'm not into country music, but this song really gets to me, and this is how I feel today," she started playing Tim McGraw's song, "Live As If You're Dying."

"Listen to the words."

Drew listened to the country story of a man who came to realize that he should live life as if every day was his last. That to get the best in life you have to maximize every day and put regrets far from you.

"That's beautiful, DeNita. Put that on repeat for a while."

As the song began to play again, DeNita said, "From what we learned today, what should we be doing right this minute? Surely it's not regretting things. And all we have is right now, Drew. What are we going to do?"

"We are going to thank God we are alive."

"Okay, let's do it."

"God of heaven, thank you for sparing our lives and so many others that survived today. Thanks for letting DeNita tell me not to be angry and dear God, thank you for DeNita."

"Heavenly father, I want to thank you also and please help those less fortunate to cope. I thank you for Drew also. In Jesus name, amen, dear God, amen."

Drew picked up the remote and clicked off the TV.

"I really don't want to hear the story again."

They lay there listening to the song play over and over and over.

Finally Drew rolled on his side and started kissing DeNita softly across her face, "Would being with me be too much for you right now?"

"All we have is this moment, Drew, and if it were my last one I'd rather live right now as if I was dying. I want you to make love to me like you will never see me again and I don't want either of us to ever forget this moment."

She put her hands on his face and pulled him closer. Each kiss, each touch, got deeper and deeper.

"I didn't know how much of my heart you had until today..." he whispered, before he could say anything else she breathed, *"I'm going to take care of your heart."* They exchanged kisses like they were cast in a desert for weeks and had just found a well. There was not one part of her that he did not explore and he was as gentle as a soft rain. He placed her under him and exchanged the pain they had experienced for peace with every passionate thrust. Everything about him satisfied her. They gave so much of themselves away that they felt it when their souls linked. Breathing and sweating were so deeply intense. Then in one moment they reached as high as they could go together and all you could hear after that was waves of sensual intimacy.

Drew was so spent he could barely utter, "I love you, DeNita."

But she heard it and responded, "Te amo."

They exhaled deeply and were sleep within minutes.

After the massacre, the wheels of justice knew they had to spin in another direction. Too many people had resigned or were in process of doing so. Drew had even typed his letter, and it was only one click away from being submitted. Somehow he knew if it did not get better than this, what was his point for being in the system? He had dreams of the glories of law helping the underdog. What he had experienced was that justice was legally blind. But not in the sense that it is taught in the law books; instead it is blind so that corruption would prevail. That was not the promised land Drew had worked so hard for. Now, after having faced losing his life for the sake of the people, he was slowly concluding that it was not worth it. His sense of personal loss was so deep that only a progressive change would save him and his career. The system finally had to face that the old way of doing things and denying advancement opportunities based on negative racial motives would have to be put aside for the common good if only for the moment.

The state Supreme Court ruled that the effective representation of indigent people was being compromised because of caseload burdens. An order was issued that no trials continue until more efficient and acceptable levels was reached. The Missouri legislature had an emergency session and paid for the complete revamping of the system.

Calvin Row finally got a well-deserved promotion. The legislature began a new department called the Capital Litigation Unit, and Row was appointed the director. This unit was especially designed for defendants for whom the state was seeking the death penalty. Other states had it. Now Missouri was stepping into the present.

"Congratulations, Row!" Drew said, "That letter did something, huh."

"Yeah it did. But you know what? It really helped me to get my fight back."

"I know."

"You want to join me in the new position. I can hire a litigator. It will be a promotion for you and it will be a lot more money which I know will help with the law school debt."

"You're right. I don't even have to think about it, man. Put my name on the dotted line. I am ready to get out of here. This is lifesaving for me."

Drew was in training for the Capital Litigation team for weeks. The training was very difficult, but Drew welcomed the challenge. It gave him the opportunity to heal from the trauma and just have a well needed change of pace. He missed DeNita and had promised to take her out for a celebration as soon as he had an opportunity. That day finally arrived. He called her on her cell phone, and they were ecstatic to talk to each other.

"I have a surprise for you," Drew said.

"What?"

"I called Chapman's Restaurant and they are going to let you sing, even though it is Friday and not their normal karaoke night. I heard that you have brought the house down."

"Drew you remembered, oh that's so sweet."

"There is nothing that I don't remember about you."

"You are such a wonderful man. Why don't I pick you up this time?"

"Okay, how about around seven?"

"That sounds good. I will see you then."

Drew and DeNita arrived at the restaurant later that evening. They were dressed semi-formal. Chapman's was a very pretty establishment. It was a modern jazz club and restaurant. The walls were studded with pictures of the great jazz musicians of the Harlem Renaissance period as well as modern artists. It was also decorated with street signs of popular black historic places and huge stop lights. The furnishings were like a 1920 club. Deep tones, red carpet and dark wood walls were in different areas.

It was owned by a black man who was well established in the community. He used the building for more than an eating place. It was a community hub, a meeting place, and he offered various black history programs throughout the year to encourage African Americans to stay connected to their past and make something of their future. He opened his place to youth once or twice a month for song night, and that is how DeNita began coming.

Drew and DeNita saw a few people that they knew. Had a few casual conversations and then sat down at a booth and ordered their meal. He had so much to tell DeNita about his training.

"You know, there is an entire science behind defending against death. What intrigues me is that everybody is trying to find a way to make sense of the duty to defend. But there never can be just one way about it," Drew said.

"You amaze me because I don't understand how you can defend people that you know are guilty."

"But that's just part of the job. Everybody has the right to a fair trial. What I am learning are many ways to defend against death and finding reasons not to kill is pretty intense. And you have to realize that there are a lot of innocent people that face the death penalty. My job may require me to be there for those who are guilty, but my heart is for people who are innocent and being thrown to the lions."

"Have you ever had a difficult time with taking a case of someone that you knew was guilty?"

"I've had a lot of those DeNita. At first it was very painful to do. But you have to learn to separate who you are from the job you are paid to do. Sometimes it is still hard, but becoming calloused in certain regards is helpful. It's like my father's hands. They were so hard after becoming calloused from years of working on railroad ties. He never could have done his job if his hands had not cooperated to callous for him. That is what helped him to lift his load. With me, I have to callous emotionally in certain areas to do this type of work. Being with you is very important to me because it keeps me balanced. It keeps me remembering that there is a softer side of life."

She leaned across the table and kissed him on the cheek, "Thank you."

"My worse case where I defended a person that I knew was guilty and got him off was a man that beat his infant to death with a bat. That was traumatic for me. I've had others like assaults, murders and domestic violence situations."

"Would you ever turn somebody down who requested your services, and you knew they were guilty?"

"I haven't yet because I realize that is the nature of the job. If I stopped defending people that I knew were guilty that would be such a large percentage that I would not have a job, but in capital litigation I might have to because I realize that for every murder case I will leave a part of me behind. And I don't know how far that will take me. I need enough of myself to live a normal life. Capital litigation charges are pretty severe, meaning that the natures of their trials themselves are more than likely heinous. That's enough about me. This change has done me a great deal of good since the Waters shooting, but how are you holding up?"

"I didn't realize that I really needed to take a good look at my life...to kind of set my priorities in order and to find peace with my past so I can move on with my future. You know I pretty much live for the company and had to ask myself if I had died what would I have accomplished. It was sort of like when Blake Adams died. He lived, did a great job, and then died—just died. Then I thought about you and how that one incident made me love you even more. I wish it did not take that to make me become that transparent, but I was hurt once and told myself I would not give that much of myself away. But when I faced losing you, it made me realize that I am wasting time not giving all of myself away because you never know how much time you have left. This has been quite an experience."

"Who hurt you?"

"A guy named Curtis, a long time ago. At this point it is really hard to determine who hurt whom the most—but I walked out on him, and I've always wondered what that did to him."

"You regret leaving him."

"No. I just never meant to hurt him like I know I did."

"You want to talk about what happened?"

"We were supposed to get married, but I left town two weeks before the wedding and never went back home. That's how I got to St. Louis. I finished up school, found work and, um...just got busy. I told my family not to let him know where I was, and they did not. But I do know he made several attempts to try to locate me."

"You know there are some things in life that you can't fix. Sometimes you have to leave them in the past. I deal with people every day that wish things had not gone as they did, but life happens. You pick yourself up and you move on. I'm sure he found somebody else," Drew reached over and squeezed DeNita's hand. "You found me. You had a happy ending. I believe that there is someone for everyone, and when you left, you just gave him an opportunity to find that person."

Just then they heard an announcement. "We have a special

guest tonight. Let's give it up for our very own DeNita Melrose."

"Oh they are calling you," Drew said.

The audience was applauding and doing cat calls. DeNita had been a part of Chapman's for a while and was well known there. The people always encouraged her and enjoyed her singing. DeNita was so happy. She smiled as she walked to the microphone.

"I have two songs for you to enjoy this evening. Okay, I am ready."

As the music began to rise she said, "I am dedicating this song to my Lord and Savior Jesus Christ." The audience applauded again loudly. She belted out the contemporary song "When I Think About the Lord" with so much power that Drew was sitting across the room with tears rolling down his face. Her entire body was expressing the song. You could feel the power in the atmosphere. It was a very spiritual moment. People in the audience were responding as if they were in church. When she began to sing the chorus people who knew the song stood up and sang it with her:

Makes me want to shout, hallelujah, thank you Jesus Lord you're worthy of all of the power and all of the glory and all of the praise.

Makes me want to shout, hallelujah, thank you Jesus Lord you're worthy of all of the power and all of the glory and all of the praise.

The melody from the chorus just continued until the music faded away. She got a standing ovation. She was so emotionally charged that she could barely introduce the next song. She was fanning her face to keep the tears away.

"My next song," she tried to start, "My next song is devoted to our Defender, Drew Jones." People turned around to find him in the audience and just started clapping. DeNita started preaching, "How many of your babies has he kept out of jail?"

"Yes!"

"How many of you in here knows somebody that he has helped?"

"Yes!"

"Has he been cleaning up corrupt law enforcement ya'll?"

"Yes!"

They were having church in Chapman's that night. Drew was so stunned at what DeNita was doing that he just sat there mesmerized with his hand over his mouth."

Then she shouted like a rock star, "Let's give it up for DREW!!!!"

The audience exploded and he did not know how to respond. He was somewhere between blessed and embarrassed, because Drew really did not like to draw attention to himself. It just came along with what he did.

They dimmed the lights in the background. She could no longer hold her tears. She wiped them away and then came out with the old school Whitney Houston's "You Give Good Love to Me." You could see people all around the audience smiling. Drew was in tears. She came off the stage, put one arm around him and sat on his lap still singing; he just melted. He just closed his eyes and leaned on her. *For a brief second she pushed the microphone away and whispered, "I hope this is okay," he whispered back, "I'm loving it."* She just sang her heart out until the song died away.

Drew took the microphone, laid it on the table and just started kissing her passionately. Neither one of them heard all of the clapping. Nor did they see all the people standing around them. They were just into each other.

Someone from audio came over and got the microphone.

"We need to go home," Drew whispered. The people were still clapping.

They got up and left. They never finished their meal.

Chapter 16

Payton Hill and Drew were about to face off again in court. This was the first time that Mr. Death Penalty himself was in the arena with Drew since the Don Henderson case when Drew literally embarrassed the Prosecutor's Office and made Payton Hill look incompetent. He had not forgiven Drew for the fiasco and hated his new public reputation of almost sending an innocent man to death. *Drew recalled passing Payton Hill in the courthouse shortly after the Henderson trial. "You will pay for this one," Payton Hill announced. "What?" Drew responded, "Pay for doing my job? You knew about the Henderson investigation, you just didn't think I would find out."*

"I don't like being publicly humiliated."

"Then don't put yourself in that position." Drew proceeded to walk past Hill and smirked, "Maybe you should have hired me in the beginning. Oh, I forgot, you didn't have any openings available." Payton just glared at Drew.

This was Drew's first case in the Capitol Litigation Unit. He was going to test his new training on defining reasons not to kill. And if there was ever a good time to do this, it was now for Antonio Rodriguez, a Puerto Rican accused of murdering an elderly white woman named Constance Parker. Her nude body was left for dead after being stabbed repeatedly. Why was

Rodriguez a suspect? He had reported the crime after smelling the body, and he happened to be the apartment manager at the time. Rodriguez had a long rap sheet, yet he was given the job as a manager because no one had wanted to take the position since it was in a very dangerous area in the projects. The previous manager had been robbed and killed. He had been raised in New York and spent most of his young life in and out of prison. This made him a good suspect for the police.

Hill had already taken it to the media. "We're seeking the death penalty on this one!" he announced. "We are going to avenge the death of Mrs. Parker."

Rodriguez told Drew that he was not guilty and that he would rather die of a lethal injection than spend another day in jail. He pleaded for his life.

Drew dug into the case with pit-bull tenacity. It was a long unfolding trail that led him from the county jail of St. Louis to the five boroughs of New York City. He discovered a dark past for Rodriguez—theft and drugs. But within those pages he found reasons not to kill. Rodriguez was a society misfit who never had a chance. He was abandoned by his birth parents and abused by his foster parents. He dropped out of school in the tenth grade and medicated his pain with drugs. He had not displayed any propensity to kill in the past. Drew just bet this would be a good foundation for his reasons not to kill. In a strange way, it even reminded him of the victim; Constance Parker was a society misfit too. No one even attended her funeral. These two lives did matter, but who would care? Drew did, but for him Rodriguez was not going down. Not like this.

He knew he would need a new suit for this trial, for, with the ways things were shaping up since his trip to New York, this was going to be a televised media frenzy. Drew was praying for a fair judge and knew he was going to have to work magic with the jury who had already committed under oath that they would be willing to put a man to death.

Payton Hill had whipped up such a bowl of public sympathy for the "poor homeless woman and the depraved killer" that his best hope was that someone could still call things as they saw it despite the flurry of negative PR.

What irked Drew even more is that he knew that Hill's motive was not as much for the victim but for his own public image—a mere publicity stunt. It was election year, and he wanted to boost his way to top office again.

Drew recalled a recent conversation with Hill.

"You do realize that all of this media attention is going to make it more difficult to find an impartial jury?" Drew stated.

"And your point is?"

"It is going to take weeks to assemble a jury. So far they have already void dired three hundred fifty people and still can't find twelve."

"And your point is?"

"You just don't care, do you? You are not giving the public a chance to think for themselves with all of this Rodriguez bashing."

"No, you just don't get it. I intend to pin Rodriguez to this murder, but I'm not going to miss an opportunity to do damage control. My re-election is coming up. Thanks to you my image is marred."

"You brought this on yourself. I didn't make your image."

"Look, the public wants officials to show care and community concern. I'm just giving them what they want and if it helps me, all the better. So I don't care how many people they have to call to construct a jury and how long it takes them. That's just more time in front of the media for me."

After several weeks and calling over five hundred people for jury duty, they finally found twelve persons that could be as unbiased as possible so that Rodriguez would have a fair trial. The trial was about to begin. Payton Hill was doing his last performance before entering Judge Roberts' courtroom.

"We must protect our citizens at all costs even those considered vagrants. Constance Parker deserved to live until death by natural causes. Not defiled by a crazed individual."

"Mr. Hill, we notice that you will be up against Drew Jones on this case, in light of what happened during the Henderson trial…"

"What happened during the Henderson case has no bearing on what we will do in the courtroom today. I am sure that Mr. Jones has prepared himself, but we are confident that we have adequately prepared ourselves. We promise a conviction no matter what tricky moves Rodriguez's lawyer might make."

"Mr. Hill, it was reported that you have a star witness named Martin Keys can you…"

"We have no comment on Mr. Keys. But he has critical information to this case, and we feel that the jury will weigh very heavily what he states…"

"Mr. Hill…"

"No further questions please."

With his last act of public manipulation, he walked into the courtroom feeling quite confident. Flanked by two assistant prosecutors and two legal investigators who were former police officers specially assigned to his office, he was ready to go. Drew had not spent his time with media manipulation, he just methodically prepared for the case.

Judge Roberts was not happy with Hill and his entourage. Nobody walked into her courtroom ten minutes late. She called both attorneys to the bench.

"Hill, I know that you are the top prosecutor for the city, but this is my court. In my court, you follow my rules. When I set a time to appear, you better have a damned good reason not to be here. Giving an interview for the camera doesn't rise to that level." This was sweet to Drew's ear. He knew the judge was not going to put up with the dramatics. Now the playing field would be a little more level.

Hill had done an outstanding job persuading the public on the depravity of the accused. Drew knew that he had to work very skillfully to turn this image around. Rodriguez had to look human. He had Rodriguez dressed in very simple attire—no fancy suits, nothing stylish, just enough to show the jury that he was a common citizen in need of defense. Drew did not put much into the psychology of the dress of the attorney during litigation, but today his colors were power colors—a navy blue suit and a wine-colored tie. He sent a message to the jury to pay attention because this was serious; quite different from the flashy colors of the prosecutor.

The jury was everything in this case. These were some pretty serious odds to beat. First there was the public outrage over a murdered elderly white woman. Then there was the outrage that a criminal with a long rap sheet had been allowed to be a manager, exposing an entire complex to an alleged heinous criminal. Then there was the sheer gore of the crime—multiple stab wounds and a nude body.

Tremendous resources were being expended to try this case by the state. Drew wanted them to spend every bit of it, perhaps that will save other people's lives. He hated that fact that in St. Louis justice often boiled down to politics and money. At least for now Drew felt that the accused was in the courtroom of a judge he respected. That would be one strike in his favor, and two if they could see the man that he was trying to paint.

Payton Hill's opening speech was nothing short of grand political drama.

"Today I stand before you on behalf of Constance Parker, a woman who had lived her life until old age. It would not be hard to perceive that she had thought about death at her age. But it would be very hard to perceive that those thoughts included death by torturous stabbing at the hands of the accused."

"Objection! Improper argument, Your Honor. He's arguing the case in his opening statement," Drew said, thinking we might as well get this started right away because every word counts in a plea for life over death.

"Sustained," Judge Roberts said.

"Constance Parker's life was taken from her. Her home was pillaged. Her elderly body shamefully exposed. She was terrorized in her own home. She was too weak to fight off the assailant. Her money was taken. We have got to get people off the streets who commit such crimes. It is my job to prosecute for the well being of public interests. The defense will attempt to persuade you that the defendant is not the heinous person that I have described. But we have a confession of guilt. I call on you today on behalf of this tragedy to do the right thing."

"Objection! He is asking the jury for a commitment." Judge Roberts sustained Drew's objection and told Hill to move on. Drew hated ploys like this; it was a way of saying 'Hang the defendant' based on a confession that could very well have been coerced.

Drew got up and started his appeal. "Our city has indeed grieved over the senseless murder of Constance Parker. But the job we must do today is to listen to the evidence that is presented to see if Mr. Rodriguez is indeed the murderer as has been implied by the prosecutor. I need you to listen with an open mind because a man's life is at stake. I believe my client is innocent and have evidence that supports that. Constance Parker deserves to be avenged, but let's not make a rush to justice.

When Hill called his first witness, Drew knew that Hill had an objective much higher than his political ambitions for going this high up on the political totem pole. He called the chief detective of the homicide division to the stand, Captain Trey Robinson. It was a rare day when any captain appeared at trial. He was arrayed in all his gold regalia and starched white uniform.

"Captain Robinson, can you tell the jury who you are?" Hill started.

"I am Captain Trey Robinson, chief detective of the homicide division."

"How many years have you been with the division Captain Robinson?"

"I have been with law enforcement for twenty years and have served for twelve years as the chief of the homicide division."

"In all of your years with the department, have you ever witnessed a crime of this proportion?"

"No. I have never seen anything this horrific."

"Can you tell us why you made this statement?"

Captain Robinson began detailing the horrors of the crime. Each account became more and more grisly. Drew watched the jury and saw the look that he wanted. He wanted them wrapped up in every word that Robinson spoke. Hill turned and pointed to the defendant. "Do you have any knowledge of Antonio Rodriguez?"

"Yes, I know that he has a long, outstanding criminal record."

"Objection. Improper impeachment, Your Honor, this is grounds for a mistrial because it is unduly prejudicing the jury."

"I am inclined to agree, Mr. Jones, and, Mr. Hill, you are well aware of this rule. I won't grant a mistrial now, but be aware I am strongly considering it! Now let your witness know I won't tolerate any further misconduct on his part. If so, he will be our guest at the jail for contempt of court. Now step back and let's move things along."

Judge Roberts addressed the jury and stated that the defendant's previous record had no bearing on the case and sustained the objection.

"No further questions."

Drew began cross-examination.

"Captain Robinson, isn't it true that your office reported over three hundred homicides last year that arguably gave St. Louis the dubious distinction of being the U.S. murder capital?"

"Yes, I heard that," said Robinson.

"Being the head of the homicide division, don't you know?"

"Objection!" Badgering the witness. Hill called out.

"Overruled, you've opened up this line of questioning," said Judge Roberts.

"I have heard those numbers," Robinson replied.

"And isn't it true that within that number you have had three children brutally raped, stabbed, and decapitated?"

"That is true," Robinson said.

"You stated that you knew of Mr. Rodriguez is that correct."

"Yes."

"Where have you obtained your knowledge of Mr. Rodriguez?"

"Encounters with him in the criminal system and documents."

"Does Mr. Rodriguez have anything on file or from your knowledge that he has been involved in violence or assaults?"

"No."

Hill glared at Drew who returned the look with a confident smirk. Drew really wanted to open this witness up some more, but he remembered the golden rule: don't ask a question you don't know the answer to. He had done enough damage making the jury see that all Robinson was there to do was to show the jury how bad the crime was. He wanted to plant in the jury's mind that this was everyday U.S.A. and just felt confident that exposing the brutality of murder and decapitation of a child would impact the jury as much or even more than an elderly homicide. Parker's murder was horrific, but in all probability not the worst that Robinson had ever seen.

"Captain Robinson, I realize that you are a very busy man and must get back to you public duties. Please bear with me for a few closing questions. Were you personally involved in any of the investigation in this case?"

"No."

"Did you write up any reports on this case?"

"No."

"Did you speak with any of the witnesses or suspects in this case?"

"No."

"Then what is your role in being here Captain Robinson? The whole city knows that this was a horrendous crime."

"Objection, Your Honor, not relevant!" said Hill.

"Overruled, Mr. Jones. Please keep comments relevant."

"Your Honor, no further questions."

The case went on for days. Each day Drew anticipated that things would get better. Surely there must be a reason for the large expenditure on this case. Yet Hill's witnesses were about the same. Very few people had little to say about the case. Surely this was a strong point in Rodriguez's favor. Drew could not put his finger on it, but there was something extremely odd going on. Surely this case was more than Constance Parker being a means to a political end. The thought that all Hill wanted was to exploit this situation was more than he could stomach.

It wasn't long before the media started to notice the show too. If this was as good as it would get the cameras would stop rolling. So finally Hill decided to display his star witness to get things going again.

Martin Keys was called to the stand. Hill started the questioning. "Would you please tell the jury your association with the defendant?"

"I knew Rodriguez as the manager of the apartments where Ms. Parker was killed."

"Did you have any dealings with the accused other than knowing he was the apartment manager?"

"Yes, we often did drugs together."

"Were the two of you engaged in any drug interaction on the night of the murder?"

"Yes. Rodriguez and I were doing crack. When we ran out, he told me that we needed to buy more dope but I didn't have any money."

"Did you stop doing drugs at that time?"

"No, Rodriguez left. He was real upset when I told him I didn't have any more money. He said he would get what we needed."

"What happened when Mr. Rodriguez returned?"

"About an hour later, he returned, and there was blood on his shirt."

"Did you ask him what happened?"

"Yeah man, but I didn't believe him."

"Objection. Speculation."

"Sustained."

"Let me rephrase that, did Rodriguez give you a reason for the blood on his shirt?"

"He said he got cut helping a tenant."

Hill continued to question Keys. He rattled on and on. Drew loved a witness who talked too much. He weaved a great story about the relationship between Parker and Rodriguez and how he knew she always kept money in her apartment.

If this was all Keys had to say, Drew knew that he was about to have his day in court. He had already investigated him and knew that he was a classic liar with a record as impressive as Rodriguez's. Hill was going to regret having under-estimated his level of expertise and, more importantly, his embedded zeal to do the right thing. He watched as the jury seemed to hang on every one of Keys' words. They really could not identify with how the drug culture actually works, but painting a picture where drugs and money gets mixed seemed to be a considerable motive for them. The media also sat on edge listening to his oratory. It was almost as if Hill had groomed him on what to say and how well to say it.

Drew stood up to cross-examine. He was about to put on a real show.

"Mr. Keys, did you kill Constance Parker?" The courtroom started buzzing. Keys started laughing.

"Man, you must be stupid."

Drew looked over at Hill. Hill was smiling as if to say, you idiot. He had no idea where Drew was going with this. He just naturally assumed nowhere. As far as he was concerned, whatever Drew could contrive would be speculative at best. Drew continued.

"Who is Miguel Fernandez?"

This took Keys totally off guard.

"I don't know a Miguel Fernandez."

Finally Hill sat up and took notice. He had never heard of Miguel Fernandez, and he knew that if Drew knew anything that he did not, that was trouble for him. The media was eating up every line of this pending upset. For Drew, this was going to be another sweet victory.

"You are under oath, Mr. Keys."

"I said I don't know him, mother fucker!"

"One more outburst like that and you will be held in contempt of court!" Judge Roberts interjected.

Hill looked as if he wanted to slap himself. He would have given anything to know who Fernandez was. "Asshole," he said under his breath. He looked over at his team of assistants. "Why didn't anybody know about this?"

Drew knew because he had taken time to find out who Rodriguez really was: a man who, through the hard circumstance of life, had become society's trash, but he was not a murderer. He was a man who did drugs, but he fed his habit by working. He did not have to murder to get drugs. He worked to get it. He was a man who at least tried to find love. He married three times looking for something that would work. Nothing in his record indicated that he was a violent man.

He also found out who the star witness was. Keys, a long-time drug user, had a record that included assault, robbery, and attempted rape. He fit the profile of someone capable of doing murder. Drew left no stones unturned in his investigations. Hill should have known better to step in court with him again. When a man's life was at risk, he would do all he could to spare it especially when he believed in the accused's innocence.

He learned on the streets that Keys had told Fernandez what really happened. Keys and Fernandez were cousins. Fernandez was well known in St. Louis for drug distribution and enforcement. Drew visited Fernandez in prison to get the whole story...

"He killed the fucking lady saying that he wanted to get respect. I told him you don't get no damn respect killing children and elderly folks. They will kill him in here because of that—the stupid ass."

"Listen, you don't have to testify all I want you to do is to show up."

"All right man. I'll do it. He didn't have to kill the bitch like that. I know that's my cousin, man, but what he did ain't right. You don't do nobody like that. He's a fool. It's hard enough to stay in this place when you did do something, but that man you're talking about didn't do nothing. This is all fucked up."

"I'm going to get you to St. Louis."

"I wish I would have had someone like you looking out for me. You really try to do your best, man." Drew could feel his eyes tearing up.

"That's the only way I know."

"I know, man; that's why I'm coming."

...While Keys was on the stand, Drew had the deputies bring Miguel Fernandez in front of Martin Keys.

"Do you know this man?" Drew said.

"No."

Hill was sitting at the table turning all shades of red. *Aw hell!* he thought.

Drew continued, "His name is Miguel Fernandez, and he is your cousin; is this true?"

"No."

Drew turned to Miguel Fernandez and said, "Thank you."

Fernandez whispered, "I want to testify."

The first witness for the defense was Miguel Fernandez. Payton Hill jumped out of his seat and objected. "Mistrial no notice for this witness!"

"Mr. Hill," said the judge, "You know the rules of evidence, no notice is required for an impeachment witness. Your objection is clearly out of place."

"I will take this to a higher court!" he vowed.

"Sustained," said Judge Roberts. "Do whatever you have to do. Proceed, Mr. Jones."

Drew and Miguel dissected the state's chief witness so well it was obvious who the real killer was—the prosecutor's star witness, Martin Keys. No other witness was called. The jury took one hour to return a not guilty verdict.

It was another outstanding upset. Payton Hill left the courthouse disgusted. The media blared the turn of events on national news declaring the black guy from the Boot Heels one of the finest and fiercest attorneys St. Louis had ever seen. Hill pushed through the crowd lips quivering with rage, speechless.

One of the reporters made it through to Drew.

"Mr. Jones, that was phenomenal. How did you know about Fernandez?"

"That's too long of a story, but in summary I did an exhaustive search for any of his associates whether they were friends or family and listened to what they had to say. Justice will prevail even if it has to come from behind bars. Miguel Fernandez had a code of decency despite his past. Just because people make wrong choices in life that causes them to be incarcerated it does not mean that they have nothing to offer. An innocent man would be locked away right now had it not been for the bravery of Mr. Fernandez. Constance Parker can now rest in peace, and so can this city. We just need to remember the less fortunate in our city and start truly doing the right thing and pursue the truly guilty." The people on the court steps and media applauded.

Calvin Row passed by Drew on the court steps.

"Hollywood," he said.

They both got a brief laugh.

Later that evening a free man came by to visit Drew's office—Antonio Rodriguez. He could hardly talk for crying. That was a surreal moment for Drew.

"I knew you went to New York."

"Yeah I did."

Rodriguez hugged Drew, "Thank you, Mr. Jones."

That night as Drew watched the recap of the trial on the news.

He also learned why Hill was trying to make the case look so much like he really cared about the public...

"*After today's stunning upset by Attorney Drew Jones, it was found that Prosecutor Payton Hill may have had additional motives for becoming so personally involved in the case. It has been alleged that he was under investigation for taking money from the Victim Services Fund to pay for prostitutes. Apparently Payton Hill was caught in the sting operation. We will provide more details as this case develops.*"

Drew remembered all too well the attitude St. Louis' finest had toward prostitution. His exposure to this left him beaten half to death on the public street and his beloved Maurita Middleton dead. Amazing how karma comes. The whole Rodriguez trial was to put a better face on the issue and to perhaps spin a few political promotions for those who testified.

It all backfired thanks in no small part to Drew Jones; this was another bitter-sweet moment for him. He rejoiced in saving a life, and showing the public not to judge before hearing the entire matter. Yet, at the same time, his heart ached as he daily watched positions that should be used for the public good turn into cesspools of misused power. Payton Hill in Drew's eyes was a horny, hypocritical bastard. No telling how many prostitution cases had been fouled up in the system due to this unethical behavior.

Chapter 17

Drew checked his voice mail for the first time this week. The Rodriguez trial had him so stretched out that there was very little time to do anything except eat, sleep, and go back to court. Of all the normal calls there were three calls from Sister Elena. That was a pleasant surprise. He picked up the phone and gave her a call.

"Still busy tearing this city up, huh?" she said laughing.

"All in a day's work. It was good to hear from you. So what brings about this call?"

"The Lord has really been putting you on my heart lately, and I called to say that I am praying for you." Drew's heart was touched. He knew if Sister Elena was praying for him then God was truly listening. He had a lot of respect for a woman who would give her life to the streets as she had. And he also knew it could only be God keeping her safe and alive in such a depraved environment. She had made such a simple statement, but knowing that someone else was standing in his corner made him feel appreciated. It had been such a hard week, and this was a good way to end it. "Just wanted to know if everything was okay?"

"Well, outside of almost being executed on the job and trying to sleep at night wondering if I'm going to be alive the next day for meddling with the way things work around here—I'll survive," he smiled.

"I heard all about that on the national news. That incident had the whole country talking, but it's all in a day's work," she reminded him. "But you know what I've come to realize about life, Drew?"

"What?"

"That there are no accidents in life. Everything comes about for a reason and God is there to see us through it all. Nobody leaves this life without His consent, and that is why I am still here and that is why you aren't going anywhere. He has too much work for you to do. You've made God proud, taking care of His troubled children. We are all his children: the best of us and the worst of us. Don't ever forget there are no accidents in life."

"Everything, Sister Elena?"

"Everything, even when we don't understand, God has a purpose and a plan. Just keep doing your good work. I'll be praying for you."

Those words meant so much to Drew. He felt like God had sent a special gift of encouragement just for him. Jeffrey Ellis had told Drew a long time ago that every murder trial takes a little bit away from your own life. Sister Elena's call was like God giving him a piece of his life back, reminding him of God's power and his purpose for him being here. It brought back his grandmother's words that he was special and that, no matter what happened, he was going to make it.

The words were as sweet as the sound of keys jangling at his door. Somewhere in the midst of all of his business, he had found time to elevate his relationship with DeNita a little more. He gave her a set of keys to his apartment. She was always a bright spot at the end of a hard day. Drew thought nothing could be better than this. Two special ladies in his life at one time, one being assigned to take care of him spiritually and the other just to be a blessing to him. DeNita had become his cheerleader, and tonight was no different. She was beaming.

"That was just masterful, Mr. Jones," she said, "But I just wasn't expecting Payton Hill to be dipping into the Victims' fund. Someone told me that he was one of their biggest patrons."

"Yeah, he was, but he was also a hypocrite."

"That's an understatement."

"Did you get a chance to see Mr. Rodriguez after the trial?"

"I did. He was very grateful."

"I know this stuff takes a lot out of you, but you've got to know it is worth it."

"I have to constantly keep reminding myself of that."

"What's going to happen to that Keys guy since he wound up being the murder?"

"The prosecutor's office has a track record of not pressing charges on people after an upset like that. They don't like being shown up."

"Even though he did it?"

"That's not my call, DeNita. That's the law, and the prosecutor has a lot of power."

"I didn't know it worked like that. But I am glad to know that Fernandez did not have to pay for something he didn't do."

"Me too, DeNita. You know I got a word from the Lord tonight to just keep going and that nothing in life happens by accident. It's all part of His plan."

"Really, how did that come about?"

"I got a call from Sister Elena, and she told me that God had placed me on her heart to pray for me."

"Wow, you haven't seen her since that Middleton situation, right?"

"Right, so this was an unusual blessing. Why are you still standing?"

"Because I came to take you out."

"Did I hear you correctly? You are taking me out?"

"Uh-huh."

"Can't get better than a date I don't have to pay for."

"Uh-huh."

DeNita could not have picked a better place to go out. She took Drew back to where they first met. It was so comforting to literally dance the night away. Their bodies simply intermingled. Drew lost count of how many times he kissed her on the dance floor. Surely heaven had touched earth that night. The only thing that he thought would make this evening more perfect was a ring.

Chapter 18

Things were calm in the Capital Litigation Unit for about two weeks. Drew was not used to this because it was always hectic in the trial office. He was right. Nothing was much different except the league he played in. This league could result in death. Then Calvin Row approached Drew.

"Hollywood, you've got to take your show on the road." Drew was being requested to take on a case back in the Boot Heels. Suddenly, his whole life seemed to flash before him, taking him back to the town that he worked so hard to get away from. It was like Moses going back to Egypt. That should never happen.

"Calvin, I don't know if I can do this. Not back home. That's a bit much to ask. I'm so burned out right now. I mean, I want too, but this might be too much for me. Sometimes I feel like I am just fading away."

"But, Drew, you don't have to crash and burn. We are going to be there for you and give you all the resources that you need. The only thing is I can't tell you if going home is going to bring you to a breaking point. You have to decide that. Drew, I've never known you to take a case where something good did not come out of it despite all the odds."

In that moment, he heard Sister Elena: *I'll be praying for you...nothing happens by accident.* He looked over at Calvin and thought how thankful he was to have him in his life. He was truly a great man in all respects, and he knew Row would honor his word. "Okay, I will take the case." So within the week he packed his bags, grudgingly left DeNita, and, like the prodigal, went home for the case the State vs. Terrance Hall.

It was a really strange feeling when Drew drove into town. Everything looked the same, but he knew things were very different. Most of his family had migrated to different parts of the state. DeMarcus, Drew's brother, was still there, but his life didn't turn out as bad as it seemed to have been headed. *Guess Grandma's prayers are still working*, he thought to himself.

The old halfway house where he had spent so many hours working was still there, though the tenants were constantly changing. Drew realized that the revolving door to the court system was always going to be prevalent in the project-ridden black community, along with drugs and cheap alcohol. These were the primary elements that kept the system fat with funding. And the Deep South racism had not changed either. It was evidently blaring. However, Drew was happy to see that it was at least blatant. In St. Louis, it was there, but in the city, it just manifested its evil in a more sophisticated way. Instead of the outright "I just hate your black ass" it was "welcome!"—and a dagger in your back. Just like Grandma used to say: *it's the same snake; it just changes its skin.*

Drew rolled up his sleeves and got to work. He met the city's chief prosecutor, Robert Madison. Drew found Madison to be quite charming and later learned that he was a prominent member of the bar, from the community, and loved by the people. Drew did his research and ended up liking the guy himself. This was such a breath of fresh air from the corrupt dealers in St. Louis.

THE DEFENDER

"Welcome home, Drew," Madison said greeting him with a smile. Looks like he had done his research too. Drew gave him a firm handshake and nodded. "Unless you can come up with a damn good reason this one will be litigated for death." Drew liked the fact that Madison was a straight-shooting attorney. He was serious about his work. No games. No motives.

"I can't plead a client to death."

"You've got to give me a reason not to because this man is evil rolled up in a teddy bear."

"All right, Madison, just give me some time."

As Drew dug into the case, he could not determine which was more sinister: the brutal death of an eighty-year-old woman stabbed over forty-seven times, dipping chicken into the blood of your victim and eating it, or terrorizing a convenience store where you worked, taking your own coworker to an isolated spot, tied, gagged and then blowing their brains out for no apparent reason. At least this is what they alleged Terrance Hall to have done.

When Drew walked into the county jail to see this potentially insane guy, he was quite surprised. He imagined him to be a strong and intimidating looking fellow, but it was quite the opposite. Madison was right. He looked like a loveable, lumbering teddy bear at six foot two and about 250 pounds. He was white had a gentle face, and you really had to focus to hear him talking because his voice was so soft. If appearance was all to it, he would have been the least likely suspect.

Drew had already done a lot of digging into his background, and he knew the scandals that would make any man already loosely hinged to snap. It always starts with a dysfunctional home, leading to constant dysfunctional choices, putting life on a collision course with destruction. The only difference was Hall's family was almost like a band of gypsies. His sad, sick tale crossed state lines from Florida to St. Louis.

"Why did you request me to take the case?" Drew said.

"I wanted someone who wasn't afraid to take on the state, was a good attorney, and was from around here."

"How did you know I was from around here?"

"You can leave town, Mr. Jones, but your roots will always be from where you left." Everybody seemed to know Drew. Hall was right: despite his big town efforts, he was from a small town. Might as well not try to hide it, but exploit it for his client's sake.

"I'm innocent, Mr. Jones. I did not do it."

"From what I've learned about you, Mr. Hall, you must be an angry man. Sometimes anger makes us do unprecedented things."

"Do I look angry? I just went to work doing my job, next thing you know I am a suspect in a murder. They do stuff like this every day around here. You've been in the system long enough to know that."

"If I was losing my home and my wife was sleeping around with all the men in town, I would probably be angry and maybe break out in ways that I should not have."

"You know about all of that?"

"Yeah, and I know every time you get settled your wife Regina does the same thing every where you have moved. Your three kids are suffering like hell because of this stuff. Life has closed in on you, man."

Hall started bawling. "I didn't want to do it, but I just kept hearing these voices telling me that he was going to be the next one."

"The next one?" Drew said puzzled.

"The next one fucking my wife, so I had to do it. I had to stop it before it happened. I just keep going through this and I couldn't take it any more. He was not going to have her. I'm tired of running, Mr. Jones. So Eric and I waited till the store closed and…"

"Eric?" Drew felt himself growing numb. That was the name of his teenaged son. It sent chills down his spine.

"Yeah man," he said blubbering, "He helped me to tie the son of bitch up, but I was the one that put the gun to his head and killed him."

Drew thought he was going to be sick. "Mr. Hall, I've heard enough. Maybe we had better discuss this some more later on."

"Are you going to help me man? Are you going to help me?"

"I've already committed to take the case. I will do what I can."

It took every ounce of strength Drew had to walk out the door. He could not fathom things in life being so bad to lead a father to take his son to help him to engage in an execution. Hall was indeed pure evil. This was the part of defense that he always hated. Drew did not tell anyone about Eric's role in the murder because he was bound by client confidentiality laws.

Immediately Drew started interviewing Hall's family. He met his sister Sharon Baines and her husband James. As far as Drew was concerned, Sharon and James were saints and as noble as people can be. You could tell she had done all she could to be a positive influence on her baby brother Terrance. Worry lines were etched across both of their faces. James had devoted himself to do anything it took to help his wife's family.

Then he met Regina, a blond bombshell. Drew knew he was standing next to poison and did all he could to keep this encounter focused and short. He never told her what he knew about their lives nor did he mention their son. She was in her mid-thirties, was braless, and dressed in a revealing white T-shirt and a pink mini-skirt. Drew assumed that was probably all she had on. She brushed past him, offering him a glass of Coca-Cola.

"No, thank you," Drew said quickly.

All he could think of was where he was and what he knew about the town he was in. He was in a city where black men were lynched, tarred, and feathered for messing with white women. He was not going to be a piece of strange fruit hanging from some magnolia tree.

He could hear his father and mother telling the story repeatedly about Wilson Black. *They tied that poor boy up to the car and dragged him though out the city for raping Martha Craft. He did not do it. There was no rape. They lynched an innocent man. God rest his soul.* It was the truth too. Martha Craft had never witnessed a lynch mob, but, when she saw what they were about to do to Wilson Black, she tried to stop them and told the truth. But it was too late; they were like sharks at the smell of fresh blood. His parents remembered his battered and bloody body swinging from the tree with the rope tied awkwardly around his tilted neck. Martha Craft went crazy after that. The last known report was that she was in a psychiatric ward in upstate New York. Her family sent her far away. The family could not endure the blemish this incidence put on them.

There's not going to be any strange fruit today, Drew thought to himself.

Drew sat intensely and listened to Regina's sordid tale. She had the psychological make up of a seriously abused woman. This was the type who would be profiled as sexually traumatized. Drew had seen enough to know she was probably a victim of incest her sexual exploits were merely a way to validate her self worth.

She also did not want anything to do with the children or Hall. Trauma would also validate why she was so removed from her family. It was truly a sad state of affairs.

"He ain't man enough for me," she concluded. "Hell no, I don't regret it; might stop one day if I ever get laid right. He said himself that he doesn't want any damn divorce *'cause like he said it's cheaper to keep her*, the old adage says. If he divorces me he knows it's going to cost him more money. But he ain't a murderer."

The evil cuddly bear was married to one as deadly as a black widow spider. This was too deadly for Drew. He kindly excused himself and headed back to St. Louis with enough data for his case.

Chapter 19

After two weeks away from DeNita, he was glad to be back. She was waiting for him...

Drew opened the door to his apartment, and it was nice to see DeNita already there. She had cooked, and you could smell roasted chicken and something that had been seasoned with garlic and bacon. Maybe green beans or some vegetable like that. She greeted him at the door and helped him with his bags. He reached out and hugged her.

"It is so good to see you."

"Missed you too, baby."

They walked over to the sofa, "So what did you cook? It smells really good."

"I saw some old recipes on the shelf in a box in the kitchen and it had Grandma written on it."

"No you didn't."

"Yes I did, I cooked Grandma's recipes."

He kissed her on the cheek and smiled, "You are so special. I thought something was odd about smelling bacon, you modern women don't know anything about soul food."

"I know it, but I do now. I had to call a few places to find out what a heaping of something was and where to find salt pork. There were a few other items in question, but I got them all."

Drew and DeNita ate dinner and talked for a long time about what happened between them over the two week period. It was fascinating for her to hear his perspective of what it was like to go back home. Drew began to recall some of the things that transpired:

"DeMarcus, I didn't know Dad and his wife moved out of the old neighborhood. I call them every now and then on the cell phone and he never mentioned it."

"It happened pretty recently, one of his wife's sister died and she left them a small house that had a nice size lot. They are planning a barbeque for you on Saturday over there."

"Was that your girlfriend I met last night?"

"Yeah."

"She seems pretty nice. You finally settled down."

"It's funny Drew, staying out of Sikeston was the best thing for you, but coming back to Sikeston was the best thing for me. St. Louis and all the women action and nightlife were too much for me. I needed someone level headed to make me do right and she's like that."

"I saw her giving you the eye last night," they both laughed. "I know she is running stuff."

"I went back to school and took up air conditioning and financially I'm doing pretty well with it. I've gotten a couple of contracts with the apartments and some businesses in the area and we are doing okay."

"That's good, man. Mama would be happy."

"I know. So what's up with you and that girl I saw on the news? That was some pretty scary stuff. I heard she was an attorney too."

"That's DeNita, and she is a wonderful person. My job can be so depressing because I am constantly dealing with tragedy and dysfunction. It is so much of it that it can be overwhelming. Don't get me wrong, I love being an attorney because I like helping people, but there is a price tag with that mission to help. So DeNita is like this big bright light that dispels my dark days. She is optimistic, lighthearted and thoughtful. I am constantly fascinated with her."

"Damn, that sounded so sophisticated, I would have just said she's got my nose wide open."

Drew drifted back for a moment.

"Anyway, DeNita, my family is doing really well. It was good to see my sister and nieces. They've gotten so big.

"So what happened with your Dad at the barbeque?"

"Oh that was nice…"

"Uncle Drew, granddaddy wants you to come outside and help him fix the barbeque sauce. He said bring the secret weapon."

"Okay," Drew walked over to the refrigerator, pulled out the secret weapon, and walked out to meet his dad.

"Go on ahead and pour it in there son."

"Drew pulled off a tab of a bottle of beer and poured it into the huge kettle that was simmering the sauce on a separate pit. He grabbed the honey sitting on the table and poured that in next, while his dad stirred."

"Oh, this smells good, Dad."

"It's going to taste even better. We are all glad to see you."

"Thanks."

"It's okay to visit home more often you know."

Drew sighed, "I know."

"We knew when you were a boy, you weren't going to stay here because you have always viewed our life as a people here being associated with such hard labor and it is hard. But when that is all people know, it's just normal and we live with it day to day with a measure of contentment. It's not shameful to make any honest living."

"I've never be ashamed of my family, Dad."

"I know, but what I am saying is there is hard labor even with jobs you gain from a book, it's just a different type of toil and I think you've found that out. So come home more okay, we miss you."

"And, DeNita, those were some of the truest words I have ever heard my father say. There is always a trade to whatever you do."

"So what do you conclude from all that, Mr. Jones?"

"That you better enjoy every day, because you will always pay a price for labor whether you have a pencil-pushing desk job like we do or you are slamming rail road ties and picking cotton. The biggest difference is your perspective of the quality of life, and I still like the way pencil-pushers live."

"Well it sounds like you had a wonderful time. Thank you for bringing back the article they wrote about you in the newspaper. It seems like you are quite a celebrity there too."

"It was nice how everyone received me, and you know I was very hesitant about going back. Calvin told me it was going to be all right. So I just used it all to my advantage to help the case."

DeNita took Drew's hand and led him away from the table and back to the sofa. She started massaging his shoulders. "That dinner was fabulous. I would have sworn Grandma was here."

"I appreciate that. She was a great cook. Anything else you want to tell me about the trip?"

"That sociopath and his relationship with his wife made me appreciate what a normal, healthy, relationship is really all about. He killed a man because he was paranoid behind her sleeping around with every man in town. She had the psychological background of an abused woman."

"That is so sad."

"All I kept thinking about is how I was so ready to go and come back home to my so wonderfully normal relationship. Can you rub that part of my shoulder one more time? It really feels good. You've been on my mind a lot."

"You know I forgot I had run you a bath. I just filled the tub up with all hot water because I was just estimating when you would get back. It might still be warm enough to get in there."

"You coming with me?"

"No, not this time, that would be too much."

Drew started laughing, "I'm the one that should be saying that would be too much."

She released him from his massage and he went and took a bath. When he crossed the hall to his bedroom DeNita was already there, undressed. He was so fixated on her that he never saw what was above his head until he lied down on the bed.

His entire ceiling was covered with helium balloons with messages like "I love you," "Welcome Home," "Thank You," and any thing else she could think of. Drew started laughing.

"What did you do, rob the balloon factory? Those are beautiful."

She smiled, "No I raided the dollar store."

"There must be a hundred balloons up there."

"Actually there are sixty-nine, and I had to make seven trips to bring them all here."

"I'm just blown away. Completely blown away."

"When I told you I was going to live my life with you as if any day could be my last I meant it. I am not going to miss one second with you."

"I don't know how I got so lucky."

"No, not lucky, you are a blessed man." She pulled Drew's head to her breasts... When torrid passion melted into sheer, listlessness two words escaped his lips: "Marry me."

She smiled.

"Being away made me realize that I need you. When I wake up, I want to see you. When I come home, I want you there. When I go away, I want this to return to. Marry me."

"That, Mr. Jones, would be my pleasure."

"I'm sorry about the ring, but this is one of those live-like-you-we're-dying moments, but I will take care of that."

"Drew, I would marry you if you put a rubber band on my finger. I've wanted this more than life."

He wrapped DeNita in his arms and exchanged one last kiss before falling asleep.

When Drew got to work on Monday morning, there were two messages on his voice mail. One was from God. Sister Elena had called again and said, "God told me to tell you he loves you and I'm praying for you." He knew Sister Elena was not a flake, so even though he was a little puzzled he took it in stride. She tried contacting him at home, but DeNita had taken the phone off the hook upon Drew's return. The second message was from Sheriff Jackson in Clearwater, Florida.

"Mr. Jones I believe the man you are defending, Terrance Hall, may be the serial killer that we have been looking for."

Drew slumped down in his chair. His entire body bristled with chills. It was hard enough on Drew to defend a person he knew was guilty after one crime, but multiple murders—this was different.

Drew called DeNita.

"Hi."

"You're calling me at work. What's the matter? Last time we did this, lunch was a disaster," she said jokingly.

"You are too funny," Drew said. "No, I was calling to say that I have to leave town for a few days on that case I've been working on. I will be in Florida. I will probably be back on Wednesday. I wish I could take you with me."

"I wish I could go. But you will be seeing more of me pretty soon anyway. I haven't been able to stop thinking about the other night."

"Me neither."

"I love you, Drew."

"Love you too."

Within a few hours, Drew was on a plane to Florida. He met up with Sheriff Jackson to hear the horrific story of a man gone mad. Listening to the events was like being trapped in an eternal nightmare; each horror story redefining gore in the most repulsive way. Six grisly murders that all happened in the same area, involving the same chain of stores, all of which Hall had worked for. This carnage started with a gunshot and escalated to a pick ax. It all matched. Drew kept his mouth shut about Eric, but it was apparent that these were not one-man jobs, and it was disgustingly obvious that he was a part of the murders.

Later in the week, Drew met up again with Hall and told him everything he had found out in Florida.

"You damn bastard, you had an opportunity to tell me all this before. This is not easy for me to do to begin with, and now you've got me tracing a blood trail back to Florida! What is your problem? You need to plea guilty and get this over for both of us."

"They will have to kill me, Mr. Jones; I'm not taking the plea."

"You know you don't want to die. You can dish it but you can't take it. It's all bravado."

The room got silent for a moment.

"You got anything else you're not telling me?"

At that moment Drew took a deep breath and looked at Hall. What stared back was Hell itself filled with demons. The soft-spoken voice oozed, "You don't know everything Mr. Jones." Drew could feel his blood boiling.

"What in the hell do you mean?"

"There are more dead than you think. I had to do it. Everywhere we went there was always somebody trying to get her ass. The voices told me I had to do it."

At this point Drew was too angry to be terrified. If there was ever a time he needed a reason not to kill it was now. This was the only time in his career that he too could hear a voice in his own head saying *if I only had a gun right now.*

"You won't try me, Mr. Jones."

"You don't know me!"

"You won't give the jury the opportunity to put me to death. That's why I need you. I did it for Regina."

Drew walked away from Hall and turned his back. He could feel his anger about to turn into an emotional meltdown. There was a very thin line between law and insanity. The law demanded that even an insane person had a right to a good defense. And a good lawyer was one who could turn his own personal convictions ice cold and side with the law. He was having a hard time turning loose the pure truth of his own reasoning and doing the job he was called to do. He turned around and looked at Hall. "I'll do what I have to do."

As those words left his mouth, Jeffrey Ellis's words were fulfilled again—in every murder trial, a part of your own life dies. This time Drew actually felt the emotional death.

When he left the county jail, his mind wrestled to find something within himself to pull from in order to develop the case. After much internal turmoil, Drew found one person worth fighting for: the faithful sister Sharon Baines. He knew it would kill her to see her baby brother executed, so he fought for Hall's life to spare Sharon. The Hall family would have done anything to have avoided what Hall did to innocent people. Drew often heard them praying their feelings for the victims when he met with them. He hated seeing them so grieved. Yet they loved their brother and would not give up on him. That was a worthy cause, and one he would never regret doing. This was the life of a defender. A good one would be a sentinel no matter what, and a serial killer is as bad as it gets. Drew Jones was a true defender.

Like the saint that he was, Drew rolled up his sleeves again and got to work. By the time he was finished with his show, he knew that Prosecutor Madison would be calling him up, reducing the sentence to life without parole instead of death. So he whipped up the media painting an image of an insane person. Surely he could find some sympathy for a man who was literally crazy. Then he played every race card he could find stepping way back to the days of Martha Craft and the lynching, just to remind the city that everyone is a little insane (including some of your grandparents that were part of the mob.) He screamed loud and clear for everyone to hear it: Terrance Hall does not deserve to die.

Then he reminded the legal system how they had abused his client's constitutional rights and brought civil suits against the jail and city. Drew was in rare form. He scrutinized the food they served to improper medical treatment. Though public opinion could not be swayed much because of the fact that this was a serial killer, Drew did enough damage to make Madison reduce the sentence. He called Drew up, "You win. We won't prosecute to death."

Hall declared Drew as the most brilliant attorney ever. Though Drew liked to win, this was still hard, another bittersweet victory. Now he had to convince Hall not to go to trial but to just take a plea.

"You know I can't win this case," Drew said to Hall in their next meeting.

"Of course, but it's going to be a great trial." This man really was insane. In Drew's mind he had done his job. He had spared a man his life. Now he needed to return to his own world where he was only one ring finger away from getting a beautiful commitment for life. *It's time for me to go,* he thought to himself.

"Mr. Hall, there are a few serious matters you need to consider before we invest in a trial. If you plead guilty, you already know you will get life in prison, but if you continue on you're going to cause a lot more pain to people that you love. I think you will want to end this when you see what I'm talking about."

He opened the door, and Sharon stepped in. With one look at his sister, Hall began to weep. "I'm sorry, Sharon. I didn't think how bad this would hurt you."

"It's all right, baby. You did some terrible things, but we still love you. You will always be family." Hall could not contain himself. "Baby, you need to listen to Mr. Jones. 'Cause we all need to be okay, and I won't be here very long."

"What?" Hall said trying to gain some composure.

"I told Gina, if anything happens to you or her, James and I will take the kids."

"What?" Hall said again.

"I have cancer, baby, and they've only given me a few months to live. To see you on trial will be too much for me. You hear me? You need to listen to Mr. Jones."

Then the flood gates broke. They both cried a thousand tears. Drew was so spent that he did not have any more tears to cry at the moment.

As he watched the two of their lives colliding in pain, he softly walked over to Hall and said, "Eric will be an accessory to murder if you go on, and in Missouri, they will kill him. There is also a good chance that he will be indicted in all the other states as well. If you want to keep your family intact, the time to do it is now. There will be no other time."

"All right! All right I will do it. I'll plead guilty. Sharon, I'm so sorry." They both hugged and cried some more. Then Hall turned and hugged Drew. "Thank you for everything. I know I didn't deserve it, but thank you."

Drew left out of there that day being grateful for what he had accomplished. He had spared a life, kept an entire family from disintegrating and given peace to a woman who was on her way to face death. The pleas went well, but it took everything out of Drew.

It was going to be a long ride back to St. Louis that night. There was just too much heartache for him to dwell on. He felt a sense of completion but also utter sadness. There was a joy in having the experience of commanding respect in your own home town and being given the opportunity to deliver justice in your own way and even experiencing some change. So many people who had cheered for him as he grew up declaring he would be a lawyer one day saw their hopes fulfilled. But the thought that he had to return in order to defend an act that was against his own conscience was a devastating blow. But who else would have fought for Sharon and the children, because surely Terrance Hall deserved death and it would have been so easy to feed him to a salivating jury? Then the most important people in his life, his mother and his grandmother, did not live to see their son return home for even this measure of victory.

It was truly a haunting feeling. Drew's eyes started to burn so badly that he could hardly see the road. He pulled over and allowed the surge of emotions to flow. He cried hard. Every tear was for all the defenders who ever laced their shoes with the intent of doing good work and what they had to put up with every day. He cried for the victims of crimes as well as the perpetrators because if their lives had not been so battered and bruised themselves they would never have the mind to commit such heinous crimes. He cried for the dysfunction, which always seemed to end in a circle of violence. He cried for his mother and grandmother. Their child had done well and returned. Yet they weren't alive to see it.

Drew looked up and saw a state patrolman's car lights flashing in his rear view mirror. The officer exited the car and asked if everything was all right. Drew tried to muster a smile and said, "Yes, officer, everything is fine. It's just that someone died today, and I'm trying to pull myself together. Thank you."

THE DEFENDER

The officer nodded and went back to his patrol car. Drew looked down the interstate thanking God that there is always hope for tomorrow.

Chapter 20

When Drew arrived back to St. Louis, it was about eleven at night. He opened his front door, and the intoxicating sent of DeNita's perfume filled the room. He also smelled the faint scent of candles that had been blown out. He called out, but there was no response. He walked past the kitchen and saw a plate wrapped in plastic and a note attached.

I waited as long as I could but I had an emergency business trip. I'm taking the last flight out to Boston, a cab will be dropping me off and I will be back on Sunday on flight 682. Please pick me up at the airport at 7:00 P.M. in baggage claims. Enjoy your dinner: my version of your favorite Chinese. Miss you and love you—DeNita.

That was the first smile he felt cross his face all day. He popped the plate in the microwave and shifted his focus on her. Even though she was not there, her powerful presence could be felt in the house. Warm memories of her began flooding his mind. It was a perfect ending to a very exhausting day…

Drew had reached celebrity status again when he returned to the office. Following the trail of a serial killer was pretty big around there. It's odd that even murder can be sensational when it's ghastly enough. Although everyone was curious about what it felt like to be in a room with someone capable of doing multiple atrocities, Drew really did not want to discus it.

"Outstanding job!" Calvin Row said while approaching Drew's desk.

"It was a nightmare. The trail of a serial killer is as bad as it gets. He wasn't the typical cold-blooded killer either. He was a blubbering big guy. This must have been part of his cover," he responded.

"You went all the way back to that old school with the lynching thing."

"It was true, and Martha Craft is still in an asylum."

"How's DeNita?"

Quick impressions flashed in Drew's mind when he said that—one steamy kiss, one passionate embrace, and one memory of ending ecstasy. "She's good. She had to leave yesterday on a business trip but will be back Sunday."

"Looks like you two are getting pretty serious."

Drew smiled. True to his character, Row remarked, "Just make sure I'm the best man at the wedding." He tossed Drew's new assignments on his desk, smiled, and walked away.

The weekend could not roll around fast enough for Drew. He left the office on Friday with a one-track mind—DeNita would be back on Sunday, and he had from now until then to clean up his wedding proposal. "I don't know what I was thinking," he smiled to himself, "No, I was not thinking; I was half out of my mind. This is one proposal story that I won't be able to share with anyone."

He headed for the mall to find a ring, and the choices were overwhelming. Finally he settled on a set. It was simple but elegant. The wedding ring was a band of diamonds set in gold, and the engagement ring was a gold band with one oval-shaped diamond. He had the words "Forever Drew" engraved on each ring. Though the price had completely burned a hole in his pocket, since he intended to do this only once, it was worth it.

Drew rehearsed in his mind over and over what he was going to do at the airport. Even though she had already accepted, he just envisioned seeing that smile over and over again. Just the thought made him feel fantastic. He could barely sleep Saturday night. But somehow he managed to get a few hours of sleep in.

Sunday was a complete blur until he left for the airport. One more time he rehearsed what he was going to do. He parked the car and scurried down to baggage claims. He scanned the area eagerly for her. He scanned the carousels to see which one would contain her luggage. To his surprise, it was at the other end of the terminal. He pressed his way through the busy crowd just to arrive as people from her flight 682 were heading towards the carousel. One by one, they grabbed their luggage and disappeared through the masses of people. Drew carefully surveyed the area and did not see DeNita.

He stayed until they shut the carousel down and reloaded new flight information. *Where is DeNita?* he thought, *I know I did not miss her. I was here early.* So he picked up his cell phone and dialed. The voice recording picked up: "Hi, this is DeNita Melrose Jones. I will be out until Sunday. I will return your call as soon as possible." Those words encouraged his heart, but he was beginning to become concerned because after several calls she did not answer.

He went to the information desk and had her paged.

"Mrs. DeNita Melrose-Jones, your party is waiting for you in baggage claims."

They announced this several times within the hour. He tried the cell phone one last time. Finally he went to the ticket counter.

"Listen, I am trying to locate someone that was scheduled for flight 682. I've been here for about and hour and a half and can't seem to locate her."

"What is her name sir?"

"It is DeNita Melrose."

"Just one minute, sir." The ticket agent rapidly began clicking in information. "Sir, Mrs. Melrose was scheduled to leave on the Wednesday 10:30 PM flight 682 and return today at 7:00 P.M. on flight 682."

"*Was* scheduled?" Drew said very cautiously.

"Yes sir. She never got on the flight."

Drew felt his knees buckling under him. "Are you sure?"

"Sir, for security reasons we now scan picture IDs for every person boarding or exiting the plane. There is not any ID scan for Mrs. Melrose entering or exiting the plane. You can not load or exit a plane without an ID."

"Could she have missed those flights and taken a later plane?"

"The system that we now use cross checks all IDs from any flight because occasionally that does happen. She is not in our system for any flight."

"Thank you," he said nervously.

He managed to find his way to the nearest chair and dropped into the seat. Drew felt his body going into shock. He pressed his face into his hands. His mind was racing, and his heart was pounding so hard that he knew if he did not calm down it would stop. He could feel the sting of tears down his face.

Oh God, what's happening? he thought. The worst thought he had is that his own cases had compromised DeNita's security. He had done enough damage to the court system that he was anybody's enemy, and he knew they were capable of striking with a vengeance. Then for just a moment between all of the chaos that was in his mind at that very moment he could hear these words of Sister Elena: *God told me to tell you that he loves you and I'll be praying for you.* He broke.

End of *The Defender*
Volume 1

For more information on *The Defender* series or other legal needs, contact:

Herman Jimerson
Jimerson Law Firm, P.C.
225 S. Meramec, Ste. 508
Clayton, MO 63105
314 862-0069